WALKING THE WALK

LAURA WARE

To my husband Don
Thanks for walking with me

ACKNOWLEDGMENTS

As always, there are people to thank for this latest collection of mine.

Dean Wesley Smith, for his continued support and help with the cover design and blurb.

Tina Seward, who looked over the manuscript to save me from myself. Any errors that remain are entirely my fault.

There are numerous Christians I know who have shown me how to walk the walk. You might never know it, but your example does matter.

My Scribes Night Out gang, who have heard me read a few of these stories and offered encouragement.

And God, without whom this collection would not exist.

INTRODUCTION

If you've been a Christian for a bit, you might have heard a version of the slogan, "Don't just talk the talk, you have to walk the walk."

The meaning is relatively simple: Christianity is a life to be lived, not merely something we pay lip service to.

It's easy to say. But it's not always easy to do. The Bible warns us that walking as Jesus did will be difficult at times. It takes effort. And making good decisions.

The short stories in this collection are not about perfect people. They are flawed. They have struggles. Each of them is faced with the challenges of walking the narrow road. They must overcome temptation, fear, and reluctance to do the right thing.

In "Choices," a preacher living in Florida in 1961 must decide whether to break the law or refuse to help out a young interracial couple who want to get married.

"At the End of the Day" tells of a church secretary who finds herself navigating a dire phone call from a young lady who needs help.

In "A Test of Faith," a physician's assistant finds herself in hot water after praying with a patient.

"The Size of Grace" explores the struggle of one who is covering up a past sin and now risks it coming out into the light.

And "The Road from Hell" gives us a grieving mother asked to do the unthinkable – forgive the man who killed her only child.

My prayer is that these stories will give you the courage to walk the walk yourself. So, let's get started. Turn the page and see how Christians walk the walk.

CHOICES

When he heard a knock on his office door, Joe Winters quickly swallowed the bite of egg salad sandwich he'd just started on. "Come in!" he called out, wiping his mouth with the napkin Dorothy had included with his sack lunch.

The door opened and a young man with unruly blond hair stuck his head in. "Preacher Joe? Can I come in?"

Winters nodded. "Of course." He switched off the radio, and the newly sworn-in President Kennedy fell silent. "Have a seat...Hank, is it?"

"Yessir," the young man said. He was dressed in a dirty blue work shirt and tan corduroys. He did not take the offered wooden chair but stood behind it, shifting his weight from foot to foot.

Winters ran what he knew of Hank through his mind. The boy's family were members of the congregation here at the 5th Avenue Church of Christ, but Hank hadn't been showing up for services the past few months. His father had mentioned his concerns to Winters but the preacher hadn't found time to visit the boy.

Now here was an opportunity.

"What can I do for you, Hank?" Winters asked, pouring himself some coffee from the bright red thermos he brought from home. "I haven't been seeing you around much."

Hank ducked his head. "I know. I been doing wrong, Preacher Joe, and I want to make it right. But I need your help."

Winters put his cup down and leaned forward. "I'll be happy to help, son." Hank's eyes darted around the small office. Winters watched as the young man scanned the bookcase on the right that was crowded with commentaries and other scholarly works. The window behind Winters gave a view of the small front lawn of the property and its red-and-white sign that gave meeting times. Afternoon traffic whispered by as the silence in the office grew.

Swallowing, Hank finally looked back at Winters. "I gotta get married."

Winters tried to hide his surprise. "I don't understand."

Hank ran his hands through his hair, making it stick out more. "I—I got a girl pregnant, Preacher Joe. I know it was wrong, but we wanna make it right. For the baby."

A baby. Oh, no. Winters bit back the harsh words that rose to his lips. Hank should have known better. But the lecture could wait for the moment. "I take it you've both ruled out giving this baby up for adoption?" he asked.

Hank shook his head. "This is my problem. I ain't givin' it to nobody else."

Winters sighed. "Hank, I appreciate that you want to do what's right, but a marriage started off like this has a heavy burden. Do I even know this young lady? I would want you both at least to get counseling."

"Why?" Hank asked. "God wants us to be married. Ain't that what the Bible says?"

If only it were that simple, Winters thought to himself with an inward sigh. "Yes, the Bible does talk about marriage. It is a serious commitment, Hank. Can you support a family?"

"I got a job," Hank said. His eyes darted to Winter's face, then to the window, as if the occasional passing car was fascinating. "Preacher Joe, we gotta get married. That's what that baby needs, right?"

Winters considered the options available for the couple as he took a sip of coffee. "Who is this young lady, Hank? I'd like to speak with her before making any decisions."

The young man bit his lip. "She—the doc said she has to stay in bed. He said she could lose the baby if she didn't."

"All right," Winters pulled the spiral bound notebook he'd been writing in as he worked on his sermon toward him. "What's her name and phone number? I could call her."

Hank wrung his hands together. "Preacher Joe, I—I guess you gotta know somethin' about Nellie."

"I do," Winters said, struggling to be patient. "I need a way to contact her, Hank."

"That ain't what I mean." Hank stared at his feet for a minute. When he looked up, he was tense. "She was a maid at the Vinoy Hotel. Before she got pregnant."

"Hank, what does that have to do—" Winters stopped, his thoughts racing. He'd never been to the Vinoy—it was too expensive for a preacher and his wife—but something about Nellie being a maid rang warning bells in his mind.

As he put two and two together, he stared at the young man across from him with an air of disbelief. "Hank, are you saying Nellie is *a Negro?*"

"Yessir," Hank said, nodding his head so hard his hair flopped onto his forehead. "She is."

Winters stared at Hank, unable to contain his shock. *What had the boy been thinking?* A stupid question. He could guess Hank hadn't been using his head. *This is a disaster. I have to keep Hank from making another huge mistake...* "Hank... don't you know it's against the law in Florida for you to marry her?"

Hank stared at him. "But...but she's havin' my baby. I gotta marry her, Preacher Joe. That's what God says to do."

"I know, Hank, I know. But you don't understand how difficult the situation is," Winters said. He considered his next words. His gaze went to the phone that sat on the corner of his desk. "I could ask around, take up a collection for you to travel up north. There wouldn't be legal problems there."

Hank shook his head. "The doc says she can't travel. And I gotta job here. I can take care of her. She don't want to leave her family anyways."

Winters blew out an irritated breath. He cast a longing look at his egg salad sandwich, which sat on its wax paper wrapping waiting for him to get back to it. "Hank, I appreciate you want to do what's right in the eyes of God, I really do. But surely you could wait until she was able to travel..."

"Why?" Hank said. "Don't the Bible say you oughtta do what's right now? What if somethin' happens to me? I want Nellie to have my name. The baby should have my name."

God, help me. A white man's name on the birth certificate? Doesn't he understand how many problems that would cause for him, the girl, the child? "The marriage won't be legal," Winters said. "You could be arrested."

Hank's jaw tightened. "I don't care. I gotta do what God says, don't I?"

Winters rubbed his temples, feeling a headache coming

on. "Hank, do your folks know about this? What do they have to say?"

"I ain't told 'em yet," Hank admitted. "I hope they love Nellie like I do."

"And if they don't?" Winters asked. "What then?"

The young man hesitated. "Well, it'd be bad, but I still gotta do what's right, don't I?"

Winters gripped the arms of his wooden desk chair. Why did the boy have to keep going back to that? And was he right? Would God approve the breaking of the law? And where was this concern when Hank was engaged in sexual immorality? "Hank, I have to give this some thought. Give me Nellie's address and phone number. I'll talk to her. I can't promise anything beyond that."

Hank frowned. "I don't understand. And Nellie got no phone."

"Just her address then," Winters urged. "Please, Hank."

The young man muttered an address to Winters that he quickly scribbled into his notebook. "Thank you, Hank. I hope to see you in worship services Sunday."

Sensing it for the dismissal it was, the young man moved toward the doorway. He paused, giving Winters a reproachful look. "I thought you'd want to help me make things right."

Winters forced himself to smile. "I do, Hank. Just let me discover the best way to help you, all right?"

Still frowning, Hank gave a brief nod. Then he was gone.

With a groan, Winters leaned back in his chair. He looked at his lunch, his appetite for the sandwich and Granny Smith apple long gone. Pressing his fingers to his eyes he prayed, "God, dear God, what am I going to do?"

～

Winters had never been to the colored section of St. Petersburg. None of his congregation lived there and he'd never had a reason to travel there.

Now he cruised 4th Avenue South in his three-year-old Impala, looking curiously around him as he searched for Nellie's house.

The wood frame houses were mostly unpainted or had paint peeling off the front. Front yards were mostly dirt with a few struggling clumps of grass scattered about. Winters noticed a rusting tricycle on its side on the cracked sidewalk near Nellie's house.

The house he pulled in front of looked a lot like the others around it. A torn screen surrounded a narrow porch. Winters got out of the car and buttoned his blue suit coat. His black Bible in his hand, he strode to the door. He hesitated at the screen door and knocked as loudly as he could.

A dog started barking eagerly somewhere in the house. He heard a woman's voice yell "Bingo! You hush now!" A few seconds later the red door that led to the main part of the house opened and a slender colored woman stepped out. She looked to Winters to be around his age and was wearing a faded green print dress.

She looked at him through the screen door, her eyes widening slightly. "Yes?"

"I'm Preacher Joe Winters," he said, holding up his Bible.

The woman frowned at him. "What you want?"

"I came to see Nellie," he said. "Hank sent me."

At the mention of Hank's name the woman's face softened. "Hank. He's a good boy. You his preacher?"

"Yes," Winters said, somewhat relieved. "I was hoping to talk with Nellie, if that's all right."

The woman opened the screen door, glancing outside as

she waved him in. "I'm Nellie's mama. Come on in. Nellie be resting but I'll get her for you."

"I don't want to be any trouble—" Hank began but the woman shook her head as she led him inside the dimly lit home.

"It be no trouble." She took him into a room with a sagging brown sofa, a television airing some soap opera that Winters wasn't familiar with, and a blue-and-white striped wingback chair.

The woman turned off the television. "You mind sittin' on the couch? The chair's more comfortable for Nellie."

"No, not at all," Winters said, carefully lowering himself down on the couch. A scarred coffee table before him held a *TV Guide,* a half-filled ashtray, and a glass of water.

Winters watched the woman go into the back of the house and fingered his Bible, wondering what had brought him here. What could he tell this poor girl that he hadn't already said to Hank? He stared at the front of the book, the words "Holy Bible" and his name stamped in gold on it. Surely there was another way...

At the sound of footsteps he looked up. The woman returned, her arm around a young girl in a tattered blue bathrobe. Her shiny black hair was a braid down her back. Her skin was the color of coffee with cream, and despite the puffiness in her face and her obvious condition, she was attractive. Winters could see why Hank had been tempted. He'd have to tread carefully here.

She eased herself into the chair, one hand on her protruding belly. She eyed Winters, then her gaze dropped to her bare feet.

The woman fussed over her, taking a pink and white crocheted blanket and placing it over the girl's lap. "You need anythin,' Nellie? You can't be up long, you remember that."

"I remember, Mama," the girl said in a soft voice. She looked over at Winters. "But if Hank sent the preacher, there's gotta be a reason."

The woman nodded. She looked over at Winters. "Can I get you anythin', sir? I got some water or I can make up some coffee."

"Water is fine, thank you," Winters said.

The woman nodded and left the room. He realized he didn't know her name. Or much of anything else, for that matter.

He looked at Nellie. She seemed to sense his gaze, looking up to glance at him before ducking her head. One hand stroked her belly while the other sat on the arm of the chair, a fist clenched.

"Nellie—" he began, wanting to break the silence between them. "Nellie, are you all right?"

She nodded, taking a deep breath. "You Preacher Joe, right? That's who Hank said he was going to see."

"I am," he said. "I asked Hank if I could speak to you about your...situation."

Nellie's mother returned to the room, a glass filled with ice and water in her hand. She placed it in front of Winters, taking away the half-filled glass that had sat there. She went to stand next to Nellie, placing a hand on her daughter's shoulder and turning to face him.

Nellie took a deep breath. "I be pregnant, sir. Hank and I, we know what the Biblesay. We gots to get married, make it right."

"Yes, he told me you wanted to do that," Winters said. He sipped the cold water andheld the glass between his knees. "You understand the difficulty of what you're asking for?"

He saw the mother's jaw tighten at his question.

But Nellie nodded. "Yessir. But it don't matter. We gots to please God, don't we?"

Winters let his gaze move to Nellie's mom. "How does your family feel about this?"

The woman thrust her chin out. "We wish they hadn't done it. But Hank, he be a good boy. He wants to do right by Nellie, that's fine by us, sir."

"It won't be easy," Winters warned. "They're young, and not getting married in ideal circumstances. We can't ignore the race issue, either. Their lives will be very difficult. And it could be dangerous."

Nellie's mama swallowed. "You don't gotta tell us that." She looked less certain for a moment, as if the words were sinking in.

Winters shifted on the couch, hearing the springs squeak under him. "You realize that the marriage is against the law," he said. "They could be arrested."

"We know, sir," the woman agreed. "But we ain't worried about that. We can do it private, no one need to know."

"You should be worried," Winters said. He frowned, looking at Nellie. "St. Petersburg, Florida, is not the place for this. If you could go to New York, or—"

"The doctor, he said I can't travel, it ain't good for the baby," Nellie said.

"You could wait until the baby was born, go up north then. Then you could get married legally."

"No sir," Nellie said. "Hank and I, we don't wanna wait to get right with God."

Winters suppressed a sigh. This was so problematic, and the couple's stubbornness wasn't helping any.

She was staring at Winters now, her eyes filling with tears. "Can't you help us, Preacher Joe?"

Winters stared at the glass of water in his hands, wishing he hadn't come. "I want to help you, Nellie, I truly do. It's just that—"

"He scared."

Winters' head jerked up and he found himself under the contemptuous stare of Nellie's mother. She had her arms folded across her chest as she glared at him. "He no better than Brother Simon."

"I'm sorry, Mrs.—" Winters stammered.

"Smith."

"Mrs. Smith, who is Brother Simon?" Winters asked. He could see the tears dripping down Nellie's face now, and he longed to be out of there.

"Brother Simon, he our preacher," Mrs. Smith said. "Hank and Nellie, they go to him first. He tell them no. He be afraid of the Klan, what they could do to him if they found out. Or some of the young toughs here." She tossed her head. "I ain't afraid of none of them. Who you afraid of, preacher?"

She isn't far off the mark, Winters thought. He suspected a few of the less savory members of his congregation had ties to the Klan—there had been times where there'd been an incident when they failed to be at services. Winters had tried to tell himself he was being paranoid, but things were tense between the races at the moment. An interracial marriage would do nothing to calm things and could well make them worse.

Winters set the glass down on the table. He got to his feet. "Mrs. Smith, I'm just trying to think of what would be best for your daughter and Hank. Fear has nothing to do with it."

"My poor baby going to be born in sin," Nellie sobbed.

Her mother's face softened. She put an arm around the

shaking girl. "Now, then, don't you fret. It be bad for the baby. We'll figure somethin' out."

Winters took a couple of steps towards the women. Mrs. Smith stopped him with a look. "You be the cause of this, preacher. You go now. I pray God show you the right way."

Searching for something he could say to undo the past few minutes, Winters settled

for a quiet, "I'll pray for you as well."

When neither woman responded to that statement, he quickly let himself out of the house and hurried to his car, the slam of the screen door behind him echoing in his ears.

Swallowing, he stared at the house and realized with a pang that in his hurry to leave he'd left his Bible there. He argued with himself about whether or not to go back for it.

But he quailed at the thought of facing Nellie and her mother again.

Because Mrs. Smith was right. He was afraid.

He just wasn't sure at the moment what scared him the most.

"Joe?"

Winters jerked his gaze up from his plate and saw his wife studying him with worried blue eyes. "I'm sorry, sweetheart, did you say something?"

The small kitchen, with its warm yellow walls and light oak cupboards, was barely large enough to hold the round wooden table they sat at. The table itself was covered with a red-and-white checked tablecloth and accommodated not only Winters and his wife but their two teenage children as well. Worn yellow linoleum covered the floor.

"I asked if dinner was all right. You've hardly touched it."

Winters glanced back down at the two slices of meatloaf, mashed potatoes, and green beans that sat before him. Normally he'd dig into a meal like this and ask for seconds.

Tonight, however...

"I'm sorry, it's great. I'm just not very hungry," he admitted.

Dorothy tilted her head. "Is there something wrong?"

Winters didn't answer right away. Instead, he looked over at their two teenage children. Keith, the fifteen-year-old, looked as if he was eating his way through seconds while thirteen-year-old Patricia was draining her glass of milk.

Dorothy followed his gaze and nodded. "All right you two. Time to finish up. Did you get your homework done?"

"Yes, Mom," Keith said through a mouthful of potato.

Patricia made a disgusted sound at her brother. "I have, Mother. May I be excused?"

"Yes you may," Dorothy said. "You both can start clearing the table—I'll be back to help you in a few minutes." Turning to Winters, she said, "Let's go to the porch."

Despite how he was feeling Winters had to smile at the way Dorothy took charge of things. Yes, he was the leader in his family, but he had to admit that without his wife's support his job would be much more difficult.

Without a word he followed Dorothy to the front screened-in porch of the 1940's house the congregation gave them to live in. He and his wife both grabbed sweaters before going outside—even though it was Florida the nights in January could still be cool.

Once they settled together on the white porch swing, Dorothy turned to him. "Now, can you tell me what the problem is? Or is this something confidential?"

Winters considered the question while he let the

swaying motion of the porch swing sooth him. "No one has asked to keep this private, but I wouldn't spread it around."

Even in the dimness of the evening light he saw her dark eyebrows go up. "And since when do I spread things around?"

"I know," he said, "but this has the potential to cause problems for the congregation. I'm not sure how people are going to react to it."

She touched his shoulder. "It sounds serious."

"It is," he agreed. With the chirping of crickets and the occasional passing car providing background noise, Winters told his wife about the visit from Hank and his subsequent meeting with Nellie Smith.

Once he was done, there was a silence between the two of them for a moment. Then Dorothy asked in a soft voice, "What would happen if you did marry them?"

The question caught Winters by surprise. "I suppose I could get in trouble with the law if I did—I'm certain doing so would break some statute. And how would the congregation react? I could get fired, Dorothy or worse. Whites get hurt for doing less than this to help the colored community."

"That's not right," Dorothy protested.

"It's the reality of the situation," Winters said. "And we'd probably be facing it all alone."

"Maybe not," she said. The porch swing's motion had slowed. Winters pushed with his feet to get the white bench swinging again as he listened to Dorothy's argument. "Not everyone thinks the law is right. Especially some of the members who winter down here. They appear to be far more advanced in their thinking in this area."

Winters nodded. "That's true. But it's also true that some

people would have a fit. I'm not even sure how Hank's parents are going to react, and he's their son."

Dorothy played with a fold in her skirt. "Does it matter? What people think? I mean, if it's the right thing to do."

"It's a factor," he said. "Honey, it's dangerous."

"But if it's right, then shouldn't we trust that God would look after us?" she asked.

"Honey, they probably can't even file a marriage license," Winters pointed out. "That alone brings the legality of any marriage into question."

"But they just want to make it right with God. Isn't that what they said?" Dorothy asked.

"It's breaking the law," he reminded her. "God calls us to obey the law."

"But not when the law is against His will," Dorothy argued. "Didn't Peter and the other apostles tell those who ordered them to stop preaching that they ought to obey God rather than men? Isn't that how we should handle this situation?"

Winters studied his wife. "You think I should do this? Even with all the risks?"

Dorothy shrugged. "I think you need to ask what Jesus would do. And act accordingly."

"Mother!" Patricia called out from inside the house, "Keith is splashing me! The water's going all over!"

Both Winters and his wife exchanged rueful looks as they got to their feet. "Duty calls," Dorothy said with an apologetic smile.

"Don't I know it," Winters replied. He put his hands on Dorothy's shoulders and kissed her forehead. "Thanks for listening, honey."

"Always," she told him. She then entered the house, her voice already rising as she asked what was going on.

Winters stayed on the porch a moment longer, his hands stuck deep in his pockets as he thought. What *would* Jesus do? And did Joe Winters have the courage to do it?

Winters woke up late that Saturday morning after tossing and turning a good part of the evening. Yawning, he stepped into the kitchen where Dorothy was doing up the breakfast dishes. She looked at him over her shoulder. "Good morning. Would you like some eggs?"

He shook his head as he pulled two slices of bread from the breadbox and poppedthem into the toaster. "I'm not all that hungry. Toast will do me."

She gave him a quick once-over. He was dressed in navy slacks and a long-sleeved white dress shirt. "Going out?" she asked.

"Yes. I need to finish my sermon. Then I may stop in to talk to one of the elders."

"About Hank?"

Winters sighed as he poured himself a cup of coffee. "Yes. I think the leadership needs to be apprised of the situation. Hank and his family are members of the congregation, after all."

He watched as his wife rinsed off a cream-colored plate and set it in the drainer. "Have you decided what you're going to do?"

The sound of the doorbell saved Joe from answering. "I'll get it," he told Dorothy. He headed toward the door even as his daughter sang out, "I got it!"

Before he could get there Patricia was already opening the door. The television in the living room was on, and

Winters caught a glimpse of Bugs Bunny. He then saw his daughter start, as if surprised.

"Can I help you?" she asked, her voice cautious.

Arriving at the door, Winters was startled to face Nellie Smith's mother. She wore a light coat that was brown and belted at her waist. A matching brown hat was perched on her head.

When she saw him, her chin went up. "Preacher Joe? I come to return your Bible to you."

He saw the book clutched in her hands. A black purse hung over one arm and swayed as she stood there. Winters realized that she wasn't comfortable standing outside his door. He noted the slump of her shoulders and the trembling of her arms.

Patricia looked from Mrs. Smith to her father. Winters put a hand on his daughter's shoulder. "Thank you, Patricia. Mrs. Smith, won't you come in?"

"I don't want to be no trouble," Mrs. Smith said.

Winters looked past her to the street and realized there was no car there at the curb besides his Impala. "Did you take the bus here?"

"No, sir. I walked over here."

"You didn't have to do that," Winters said.

Something flashed in her eyes. "We ain't no thieves. This Bible, it belong to you. I bring it back."

"No, of course you aren't a thief," Winters said quickly. He opened up the screen door that separated them. "Please, come in. I can drive you back home after you rest a minute."

Mrs. Smith hesitated. "You sure that's okay?"

"You welcomed me into your home. Please let me extend the same courtesy."

She studied him for a moment. Then, with a nod, she

stepped inside the living room. "Maybe you're a man of God after all, Preacher Joe."

Patricia's mouth dropped open. Before she could say anything Winters spoke. "Sweetheart, I'm taking Mrs. Smith to meet your mother. You can go back to watching television."

Patricia looked as if she was going to burst with questions. But she closed her mouth and headed back to the dark green couch where she'd undoubtedly been curled up before the doorbell rang. Winters sent up a silent prayer of thankfulness for her obedience. He then escorted Mrs. Smith to the kitchen to meet Dorothy.

His wife turned to them as they entered the kitchen. If Winters' companion surprised her she hid it well. "Hello. I'm Dorothy Winters," she said, quickly drying her hands on a red-and-white checked dishtowel.

"Regina Smith," Nellie's mother replied. She looked around the neat kitchen. "This be a nice place you got here."

"Thank you," Dorothy replied. "Please, have a seat. Would you like some coffee?"

Their guest hesitated. "I don't wanna be no trouble."

"It's no trouble," Winters insisted. "Please, I would like us to talk a minute. We didn't leave things in a good way yesterday."

Mrs. Smith frowned at that, but placed Winters' Bible on the kitchen table before pulling out one of the oak kitchen chairs. She sat on the edge of it, her purse now gripped in both her hands.

Winters retrieved his cooling cup of coffee and poured another cup for Nellie's mother. He set it in front of her before taking a seat across from the woman. "Is Nellie all right?"

"Nellie's fine," Mrs. Smith said. "Hank's with her. He offered to drive me here, but I didn't want her to be alone."

Dorothy started to leave the room. "I suppose you both need to talk, I'll just check on the kids."

To Winters' surprise, Mrs. Smith said, "You can stay, Miz Winters. I got no secrets from the preacher's wife."

When Dorothy looked his way, Winters nodded. He admitted to himself he felt more comfortable with Dorothy there in this situation. Without another word his wife came and sat next to him at the round breakfast table.

A silence descended on the three of them. Their guest finally broke it. Looking at Winters directly, she asked, "You been thinking about things, Preacher Joe?"

He swallowed. "I have," he admitted. "To be honest, I'm not sure what to do here, Mrs. Smith."

"Those children need to be married," she responded. "That's what God wants."

"If they'd been concerned with what God wanted in the first place there would be no need to get married," Winters said.

Mrs. Smith dropped her gaze. "That be true," she admitted. "But we can't change what's been done."

Winters struggled to find the words he needed. "There can't be a legal marriage," he said. "They can't get a license. Anything I do would be symbolic at best. And it will cause more problems than it would solve."

"But they could be married in God's eyes, couldn't they?" Smith said, looking up to meet Winters' gaze. "Even if the law won't let them."

He sighed. "In a sense, they are married in God's eyes. The Bible doesn't give a wedding ceremony for us to follow. That is man's tradition, one we honor as we honor the laws of the land."

"They need that," she insisted. "They need that ceremony to feel like it's right in God's sight."

"And what then?" Winters asked. "They would have no legal standing in Florida. And you know as well as I that interracial couples are not tolerated in this state. You understand that, don't you? If they want to be married in the eyes of the law, they can't remain here."

Mrs. Smith swallowed, and Winters saw her eyes fill with tears. "I know. They got to go away and never can come back."

"That's true," Winters agreed. "But what is best for them? You know they won't be accepted here. Not by many whites. You mentioned that some of your people would have problems with it. Is that what you want for your daughter and grandchild?"

The woman sniffled, wiping her nose with the back of her hand. "If it's your daughter, what would you want?"

Patricia wouldn't get *in a situation like this*, he thought.

Dorothy shifted in her seat. She looked over at him. "I don't know," she said, her voice soft. "It would be hard. But Joe is right. Things would be very difficult for them here."

Winters sighed, his gaze traveling from face to face. He wished he knew what the answer was...

He suddenly had a thought. "Mrs. Smith, have you prayed about this?"

She clasped her hands in front of her. "I been praying about this ever since I learned about the baby."

He stretched a hand toward his guest. "I think we should all pray about this situation. Together. Will you pray with me, my sister in Christ?"

His gaze never leaving his guest's, he held out his other hand and felt Dorothy take it without hesitation. Mrs. Smith stared at him, considering. Then she reached out and grasped his fingers. "My name's Regina, Preacher Joe," she said, stretching her other hand out for Dorothy to take.

Winters nodded. "Let's pray, Dorothy and Regina."

The bride sat in the same blue-and-white wingback chair she'd been in the first time Winters came to visit. Instead of a tattered robe, she wore a yellow dress with a ruffled skirt that brightened up the dim living room. She clutched a bouquet of daisies in her right hand, her left firmly wrapped around the hand of the groom, who stood next to her.

Hank wore a white dress shirt and a pair of black slacks. Winters recognized the outfit from when Hank would come to church. He suspected that they were the only nice set of clothes the boy owned.

Hank shifted from foot to foot, clearly nervous. Winters could relate to that feeling.

His gaze traveled around the room, taking in both sets of parents who were eyeing each other warily. They'd just met a few minutes ago.

Winters recalled the meeting with Hank's parents that the boy had asked him to bring about. It had not been an easy time. Hank's mother sobbed for a good half hour, while his father yelled at his son, using language that made Winters blush.

In the end, he'd persuaded the Millers to his way of thinking. That the plans that had occurred to him after praying that Saturday morning were for the best. So, they had come, clearly uncomfortable, but at least supporting their child.

Winters looked over at Dorothy, who gave him an encouraging smile. They'd agreed not to tell Patricia or

Keith about this, not wanting to burden them with such a secret.

And a secret it had to be. For everyone's sakes.

Winters looked over the notes he'd made for this unusual ceremony. It was not legal. It would not stand up in court. There could be trouble ahead if word of it got out.

But the law was wrong.

Yes, Hank and Nellie had been wrong to engage in immorality. But in the end they desired to make it right. Winters, seeing only the wrong they'd done, had let himself forget that. They loved each other, they loved God, and were willing to act on that love regardless of the consequences.

Winters hadn't been so willing. He'd been too concerned about what people would think—what he himself thought. He'd forgotten what was most important—what God thought. And in this Hank and Nellie were more right than he was. God's law called for them to be married. Had they both been white, that would have been what he advised.

Why had he let Nellie's color blind him to that truth?

In Winters' mind, he was obeying God by supporting this couple's desire to be together for the sake of their child. Others might argue with him. But this was what he felt he was led to do.

In return for his conducting this ceremony, Hank and Nellie had agreed to travel to a northern state after the baby was born and get married properly. After Winters spoke with them both parents agreed, with sorrow, that letting their children leave was for the best.

Winters looked at the couple before him and sent up a final silent prayer, that someday such a marriage would not have to be kept secret in Florida, or anywhere else in the country.

He cleared his throat, and all eyes turned toward him. Committing himself to God, he said, "Let us begin."

AT THE END OF THE DAY

Jill glanced at the round wall clock that hung next to the door to her office and sighed. 2:45 in the afternoon – she had to stay fifteen more minutes.

Normally, she enjoyed her job as church secretary for the Sebring Community Church. Jill's office, which she shared with the youth minister, was quite spacious. There was plenty of room for shelves that held things like different colored printer paper, books, and printed Bible studies one could conduct with an unbeliever.

Behind where she sat stood a tall, commercial-grade printer that had so many bells and whistles Jill sometimes felt intimidated using it. The preacher, Mike, had been a patient teacher when she was first hired six months ago, but Jill was fairly certain she didn't know everything it could do.

Most days she thought she was doing some good for others in this job. She sent out prayer requests and let people know who needed help. Along with Mike, she prepared the weekly bulletin, always looking for articles that would uplift and encourage her brothers and sisters in Christ.

Sometimes people would drop in and chat. If she wasn't busy, she took the time to listen to others and share news or funny stories about her two children. As church secretary, she felt connected to the congregation, and she loved it.

But today...today had not been a good day. A number of little things had gone wrong, and they'd added up to irritate her.

First, she'd overslept, which made her rush through her morning routine and settle for a banana for breakfast. Once at the office, she'd managed to jam the copier and unjamming it had been an exercise in frustration. She had forgotten to bring some coffee pods for the Keurig that sat on top of a filing cabinet, which meant no morning coffee. And these even weren't everything that had conspired against her that day.

Jill took off her glasses and rubbed the space between her eyes, wishing her headache would go away. One of her two computer screens displayed the congregation's email, while the other was open to their website. Both had added to the stress the day had put on her.

There had been several spam emails that Jill deleted, but one email had been hurtful. A woman who was a member complained that no one, including the preacher, had visited her during her recent two-day hospital stay.

The unhappy member didn't appear to consider that she'd told no one about the stay until she was released. Jill had several talents, but mindreading certainly wasn't one of them.

She'd flagged the email and forwarded it to Mike and the elders of the congregation so that they could deal with it. It was, as she liked to put it, "above her pay grade." And if she were being honest, she'd admit the response that occurred to her was hardly loving.

She wished Mike had been there to talk about it, but he'd left over an hour ago to do some visitation of people who were ill or shut in. Robert, the youth minister, had left to spend some time with his young children. His two girls, aged five and three, were adorable and popular in the congregation, along with their youthful peers.

This left Jill holding down the fort. Most of the time it wasn't an issue. But the irritants had piled up that day, and she was ready to threaten her computer with a hammer.

The website had crashed when she'd uploaded Sunday's recording of the morning service. Of course, it happened when Mike and Robert were gone – Robert especially was good with the website – while Jill felt like a toddler learning calculus.

She glanced at her smartphone for the third time in twenty minutes. Robert lived close by – one phone call and he'd be back in the office, or even doing his magic from his home computer. At the very least he'd take a stab at talking Jill through the problem.

But he'd been away at a Bible camp with the older children all last week, and Jill knew he had been looking forward to the time today with the girls. She hated to interrupt him, even if the website mocked her attempts to get it up and running again.

She *had* tried to call Mike – but it had gone to voicemail. Jill suspected she wouldn't hear from the preacher until after she'd left the office. Granted, the website being down was a minor problem in the grand scheme of things, but it *was* a problem.

With a sigh, Jill looked at the clock again. She'd been woolgathering for about three minutes. Twelve minutes to go.

She decided she'd prepare to leave by straightening up

her desk and putting away files she'd taken out to refer to that day. Maybe by the time she was done she'd be able to go home with a clear conscience.

Jill spent the next five minutes putting file folders back into their proper cabinets and checking the congregation's email one last time for any announcements that needed to be made. She'd call Robert about the website later, maybe after the girls were in bed.

As she stood to visit the bathroom, the phone that sat on her desk rang.

Jill checked the Caller ID. It had a phone number that she didn't recognize.

She was tempted to let it go to voicemail. It had been a long day. She wanted to go home and take a nap. It was probably someone who wanted money.

The phone rang a third time. One more ring and it would flip to voicemail.

Cursing her overdeveloped sense of responsibility, she grabbed the receiver. "Sebring Community Church, how can I help you?"

A woman spoke hesitantly. "Is the pastor there?"

"No, he's not, may I give him a message?" Jill asked.

There was a brief silence on the phone. "No...I just really need to talk to someone."

Jill fought a surge of impatience. "May I ask what this is about?"

More silence. Then, in a voice so soft Jill almost missed the words, the woman said, "I think I want to kill myself."

Jill sat hard in her chair, the phone pressed to her ear. "I'm sorry? You want to commit suicide?"

"I think so," the woman said. "My grandmother died last week. She had a prescription for sleeping pills, and I took the bottle yesterday when I was cleaning up her apartment. I'm looking at it now."

Jill's heart pounded. She didn't know what to do. She looked at her cell phone, willing Mike or Robert to call her. "Um, sweetheart, what's your name? I'm Jill."

"Donna," she said. "Who are you?"

"I'm the church secretary," Jill said. She wondered if she could jam the landline receiver between her chin and shoulder so she could use her hands to text for help. Unlike her adult children, she wasn't adept at typing on her phone with only one hand.

"Oh," Donna said. "Do you know anything about God?"

"Yes, I do," Jill said. She wondered if she could get someone to put a trace on the call. She nearly dropped the receiver as she reached for her cell phone. "Donna, where are you?"

"You're not going to call the police, are you?" Donna sounded alarmed. "Don't call anyone. I'll hang up, I swear I will."

Jill froze in the middle of looking for Mike's number. "Honey, you sound like you need help. They can help you get it."

"No," Donna said. "This was a mistake. I'm sorry I bothered you."

"No, don't hang up!" Jill shouted. "Please, I haven't contacted anyone. I won't if you stay on the line."

Silence. Jill could hear Donna's fast breathing. "You promise?"

Jill looked at her cell and put it back on the desk. "As long as you stay on the line, I won't call anyone. I promise."

"Okay," Donna said. "Jill, if I kill myself, will I go to Hell?"

The question was one Jill had never considered. "I – I'm

not sure. Murder is a sin, and killing yourself is like a self-murder."

"But I feel like I'm in Hell now," Donna said. "Maybe God would understand?"

"Why do you feel as if you're in Hell?" Jill asked. She took a sip from the cup of Dr. Pepper she'd bought with lunch at Arby's a couple of hours ago. Her bladder complained, but she could hold it for now.

"Because I am," Donna said, her voice sad. My grandmother died, and she was the last person who really cared about me."

"Are you sure about that?" Jill asked. "What about your family?"

"My parents *say* they care, but they're too busy to pay any attention to me," Donna said. "My dad keeps saying Grandma is in a better place now. I want to be there, too."

"How old are you?" Jill asked. She was looking for something, anything, to give her a handle on this girl.

"Nineteen."

Younger than Greg and Emily, her two children, both in college out of state. "Are you going to school?"

"No, ma'am," Donna said. "I worked as a cashier part-time. I was helping take care of my grandmother, or I would have worked fulltime."

"You're not working now?" Jill asked.

"I got so upset when my grandmother died, it was hard to work. I'd sometimes burst into tears for no reason," Donna said. "They were nice about it – said I could come back once I got over stuff. But I don't know how to get over this."

"Grief is very hard," Jill admitted. She thought about losing her own mother two years ago. There had been some difficult days. "It does get better with time."

"No, things don't get better," Donna said. "My grand-mother listened to me, made me feel special. I broke up with my boyfriend last month, and my folks just said I'd get over it, there were many fish in the sea, blah, blah, blah. Grandma understood and let me cry."

"Why did you break up with your boyfriend?" Jill asked.

Donna's voice took a shy tone. "Well, Pete, he...he wanted us to do stuff. And I'm not ready. I mean, what if I got pregnant? He said he'd use a condom, but I know those aren't 100%. He wouldn't let up about it, so I told him we were through."

Jill felt a surge of sympathy for this teenaged girl. "You have a lot to process right now."

"It's too much," Donna whimpered. "I can't handle it. They're going to have Grandma's funeral on Saturday. I can't deal with that. I want to be gone."

"Donna, listen to me," Jill said, talking quickly. "Killing yourself isn't the answer. Think of the pain that will cause your family. They've already suffered one loss – another could be devastating."

"I told you, they don't really care about me," Donna said with a sniffle. "They didn't understand when I lost my job, they said I had to grow up and deal with things like an adult. I'm doing the best I can."

"I'm sure you are," Jill said. She wondered about Donna's parents. "Hon, where are your parents now?"

"At work," Donna said. "Dad's a lawyer, Mom is an accountant. They won't be home for a couple of hours."

Jill's bladder complained again, and she crossed her legs. "Donna, I don't think you really want to kill yourself. You called here – why?"

"I drive by your building a lot," Donna said. "I like the stuff you put on your sign outside – sometimes it's really funny. I thought you might be nice people...and the pastor would know about the Bible."

"I like to think we are nice," Jill said. "And I know something about the Bible. Do you have a way you could come over here to the building? We could talk and look at the Bible together."

She heard Donna suck in a breath. "I don't know...I think I still want to kill myself, but I'm so confused now."

"Please come," Jill said. "I'll stay on the line until you get here – but is it okay if I go to the bathroom? I really need to."

"You do?" Donna asked. "Yeah, stay on the line, I guess... I don't know about coming over. You might have someone waiting to put me in the hospital."

Jill slipped out of her office and trotted around the corner where the ladies' room was. "I won't do that. I told you I wouldn't call anyone."

"I could take the pills right now," Donna said. "Would you stay on the line with me if I did? Just till I went to sleep."

Jill froze in front of a stall. "Donna, honey, please don't take any pills. Please, just talk to me for a while longer."

It was awkward pulling down her tan pants and hanging on to the receiver, but Jill managed. Donna said, "It's not your fault. No one should blame you."

Jill got on the toilet with a sigh of relief. "Honey, that's not the point. You sound like a nice young woman, and I don't want you to get hurt."

"How do you know I'm nice?" Donna countered. "My parents say I'm childish and irresponsible. That doesn't sound nice."

"A mean person wouldn't help take care of her grandmother," Jill countered. "She wouldn't care if her grandmother died. You clearly love your grandmother, to the point you didn't take full-time work. That sounds like a nice person."

There was silence on the line. Jill finished her business and got up, hiking her pants up and flushing the toilet. Worried, Jill asked, "Donna, are you still there?"

"Yes," Donna said. "Do you feel better now?"

"Much," Jill admitted. Keeping the receiver jammed under her chin, she washed her hands. "Sweetheart, if you won't come to me, may I come to you? I promise I'll come alone."

"I don't have much time," Donna said. "My mom will be back a little after five. I have to take the pills before then."

"Donna, please," Jill begged. She tried to think of a way to get the girl out of wherever she was. "If you don't want me to come over, we could meet someplace. Would you do that?"

"Where?" Donna asked.

Thinking quickly, Jill said, "What about the Dunkin' Donuts at Walmart? I'll buy you a coffee and a doughnut and we can talk. Please?"

There was a pause. Then Donna said in a wistful tone, "I like doughnuts."

"Then will you meet me there?" Jill asked.

She heard the young woman sigh. "Okay. But I'm bringing the pills. How will I know you?"

Jill described herself, down to her pants and dark blue short-sleeved blouse. "I'll stand at the entrance to Dunkin'. I'll wait for you."

"Okay," Donna said. "I'll be there soon."

Jill didn't like the thought of hanging up. "Donna, can I give you my cell phone number? You can call me on it, and we can keep talking on your way over."

"You'd let me have your personal number?" Donna said.

"Yes, why wouldn't I?" Jill asked.

"You don't know me," Donna pointed out. "I'm a stranger."

"You're someone who needs a friend," Jill said. "And I'm willing to step in. Have you got something to write with?"

"Just a sec." There was a flurry of sound, then Donna returned to the line. "Okay, I'm ready."

Jill rattled off her number, and had Donna read it back to ensure she'd gotten it correct. "All right. I'll meet you there. Please call me after we hang up."

"Okay, Jill. Thank you." A click and she was gone.

Jill started to replace the receiver, then decided to bring up the Caller ID and copy Donna's number down. If she didn't call, Jill would alert authorities for assistance. The number could be traced.

She'd just put the receiver on its base when her cell rang. A glance showed Donna's number. Filled with relief, Jill answered. "Hi."

"I'm getting in my car now." Donna's voice sounded distant. "I have you on speakerphone at the moment."

"That's okay," Jill said, grabbing her purse from where it hung on the back of her chair. "I'm locking up. See you soon."

Jill leaned against the wall at Dunkin' Donuts' entrance. She had a clear view of the entrance to Walmart and had watched several people going in and out of the big box store.

To her left she could smell coffee as people picked up their selections of caffeinated goodness and sugar rush. There were a half dozen tables along a wall and across from the counter where people placed their orders. A couple of shopping carts with items sat close to where Jill stood – the carts wouldn't fit in the dining area.

For the past fifteen minutes she'd done her best to keep Donna talking. She'd told the girl of her own children in college now, and how she missed them. Donna had an older sister, who was married and living in Ohio. They didn't sound close.

"I just pulled in," Donna said. "I'll be there in a few minutes."

"All right," Jill said. While she waited, she prayed for wisdom. How to help this poor girl see her life was worth something? How to keep her from throwing it away?

A few minutes later she spied a young woman walking into the store, a smartphone pressed to her ear. Her brown hair hung lank and lifeless over her shoulders. She wore a pair of jeans with decorative tears in them and a shapeless Princess Leia t-shirt. Her free hand clutched a denim cloth purse tightly.

Stopping in front of Jill, she asked, "Are you the church secretary?"

Jill nodded, disconnecting her phone. "You must be Donna."

Donna nodded, slipping her phone into a pocket. "What now?"

Jill swallowed. "Why not some coffee and doughnuts?" she asked, waving towards the counter. "Get what you want. My treat."

"You don't have to pay for it," Donna protested.

"I want to," Jill said. "Please?"

Donna looked at the counter, then back at Jill. "That's... nice of you."

There was no one at the counter at the moment, so the women were able to place their orders right away. Donna ordered a large hot mocha and two glazed doughnuts. Jill chose a hazelnut swirl in her coffee and two French crullers she didn't need but wanted.

It wasn't long before both women were at a table across from each other. Donna cautiously sipped her coffee. "Hot."

Jill nodded. "I know." She took the cover off her own drink and blew on the steaming liquid. "Mine too."

Donna nibbled one of her doughnuts. "I don't understand why you care so much."

Jill cocked her head. "I told you – you seem like a nice woman and I don't want to see you get hurt."

Shaking her head, Donna said, "You barely know me. But you talked to me, gave me your cell phone number. You bought me coffee and doughnuts and you don't seem in a hurry to get rid of me." She sighed. "Why would you do all that?"

"Why wouldn't I do that?" Jill countered. "Donna, you believe in God, yes?"

"Well, yes," Donna said. "I don't go to church though."

"God cares about all His creation," Jill said. "There's a verse in the Bible that says we're fearfully and wonderfully made. He cares about you, Donna."

"But you're not Him," Donna said.

"But He tells me to be like Him," Jill said. "God has been good to me and wants me to be good to others. Especially those who need help."

Donna's eyes filled. "But how can you help me?" she said. "You can't fix my life. You can't bring my grandmother back to life, or make my parents understand."

Jill felt her heart sink. Donna was right – she couldn't do those things.

Wait a second. Maybe...

"Donna, you said your grandmother's funeral was on Saturday."

The girl nodded, blinking her eyes as she sipped her coffee.

"What if I went with you?" Jill asked. "You could lean on me for support."

Donna's eyes widened. "But you didn't know my grandmother."

"But I know you," Jill said. "I want to be your friend. And I could help you get through it."

Donna sat back in her seat. "But...do you know what it's like to lose someone like her?"

Jill offered Donna a sad smile. "Unfortunately, yes. My mother passed away two years ago. Heart attack. It was sudden."

She watched Donna suck in a breath. "I'm sorry."

"I know," Jill said. "But you see, I do know something about it. Not exactly – I'm not you. But I understand you're in a lot of pain right now."

Nodding, Donna whispered. "I want it to stop."

"I know that, too," Jill said. "But really, is killing yourself the only way to make it stop? There are other ways to deal with it, ways that aren't so irrevocable."

Donna frowned. "Irrev..."

"It means you can't take it back," Jill explained. "You just want to stop hurting. There are options. Please, let me help."

Donna toyed with a half of a doughnut on her napkin. "I'm afraid. I can kind of see it, sitting here with you, but when I'm alone, all I can think about are the pills."

Jill took a deep breath. "Do you trust me?"

"I...maybe?" Donna said.

"Give me the pills," Jill said. "Let me hold them for you. If you don't have them, you can't use them."

Donna went very still. "What would you do with them?"

"I'd keep them someplace safe until you said it was okay to get rid of them. But I wouldn't give them back to you if I thought you'd use them to hurt yourself."

Donna seemed to study her for a long moment. "You'll come to my grandmother's funeral? Will you tell my parents about this?"

"Hon, this is between you and me. I think you should tell them, but that's up to you," Jill said. "And yes, I'll come to the funeral."

Donna's gaze dropped to her purse. "Will you tell anyone?"

Jill thought about it. "I'd prefer not to keep secrets from my husband, but he would be the only one. And if you tell me not to, I won't tell even him."

"What does your husband do?" Donna asked.

"He's a bank manager," Jill said.

Donna looked thoughtful. "That's okay, I guess. You can tell him."

She opened her bag and dipped her hand inside it. When she pulled it out, she was holding an orange prescription bottle that was half full.

Jill put her hand out, trying not to hold her breath. She saw Donna's hand shake as she gently placed the bottle in Jill's outstretched hand.

Jill quickly slid it into her purse. "Thank you, Donna."

The girl's eyes were pinned to Jill's purse. "Thank you, Jill. I think you're right – I need to find another way. Will you help me?"

"It would be an honor to help you," Jill told Donna.

Jill knew things were far from fixed. In some ways, Donna's needs were beyond Jill's abilities. But she could help the girl get the help she needed and support her through the rough times. That was what a friend did, wasn't it?

And God would help her find the path. She was certain of it.

Donna took a bite of glazed doughnut. "What happens now?"

Taking a drink of her own coffee, Jill said, "We take it one step at a time. You have my number – I'm just a phone call away."

Donna finally smiled. "I know that. Thank you, Jill. Maybe God knew when I should call your church, huh?"

Jill smiled, glad that she'd chosen to answer the phone earlier. If she hadn't...she felt a shudder go through her.

"You know what?" Jill said, grateful for the end of this day after all, "I think you might be right."

A TEST OF FAITH

Kathy Abrams sipped her cold can of Dr. Pepper as she used the Bible app on her iPhone to look up a verse her preacher had used in a sermon the day before. The clinic was quiet now, with everyone else out to lunch, and it was a perfect time to relax and reflect for a bit.

The break room in Doctor Bruce Gamble's clinic was a small kitchenette on the south side of the office space. A full-sized white refrigerator sat in one corner. A small counter held a microwave and a sink, with room for a dish drainer to the right of the sink. A table that could seat four if they didn't mind being cozy was on the opposite wall.

Kathy finished the last of her Walmart lunch (spaghetti and meatballs) and reached for the container of turtle cheesecake that she'd also purchased at the large store. She put down her phone to open up the plastic cup and dip the plastic spoon she'd brought into it.

Her aching feet felt better after sitting for more than two minutes. It was her first day as Dr. Gamble's medical assistant, and the man had a busy family practice. She'd been hired out of school in nearby Tampa to this clinic in

Sebring and she already loved the small town feel of the area.

The bells on the front door jangled. Kathy knew she'd locked the door behind Dr. Gamble, who'd been the last one to leave the clinic for lunch. Therefore, someone from the office had returned.

A minute later the office manager Jessica Wolf stuck her head in the break room. Like Kathy, she wore pale blue slacks and a dark blue smock. "Hey, Kathy, how's it going?"

"Fine," Kathy smiled. "I'm about finished with lunch."

"Oh, take your time, I came back early," Jessica said as she opened the fridge to take out a can of Sprite. "I see you like Dr. Pepper – I'll make sure to keep some in here for you."

"That's very kind of you," Kathy replied. She scraped the last of the cheesecake from the container and licked the spoon clean.

"Hey, anything we can do to help. You did great this morning. I like how you don't shy away from doing your job," Jessica said. "You're good with the patients."

Kathy ducked her head. "Thanks, I appreciate that." She picked up her phone. "If I have a few minutes, I'll finish my reading."

"Oh? What are you reading?" Jessica asked, popping the top of her can of soda and taking a sip.

"My Bible," Kathy answered. "Just going over something my preacher said yesterday."

Jessica frowned, pulling her soda away from her mouth. "Your Bible?"

Wondering at the other woman's reaction, Kathy said, "Yes."

"You're a Christian?" Jessica asked.

"Yes," Kathy said. "Is there a problem?"

"Maybe," Jessica said. "Look, I'll be straight with you – Dr. Gamble doesn't want any of that religious stuff in the office. He doesn't believe in it and thinks it's unprofessional. Understand?"

It was Kathy's turn to frown. "I can't even read my Bible on my lunch hour?"

"I know – it sounds extreme. But Dr. Gamble has a real attitude about it," Jessica said. "If I were you, I wouldn't let him find out you're religious. It will make your work here harder, believe me."

"But what about the First Amendment?" Kathy asked.

Jessica shook her head. "You can't go there. This is a private business, and the doctor can run it as he wishes. Look, Kathy, I think you'll be a good fit here but if you push this you might find it not so fun to work here. Understand?"

Kathy couldn't believe it. This was the United States. The doctor couldn't trample over her rights like this – could he?

"I'm sorry, I really don't get it," Kathy admitted.

Sighing, Jessica said, "It's your funeral. Don't say you weren't warned." She glanced at her Apple watch. "Patients will be arriving in about ten minutes. I've got to get ready."

"Okay," Kathy said. "I'm sorry I upset you."

"Just think about what I told you," Jessica said. "You'll be happier if you do."

After Jessica left the break room, Kathy picked up her trash and dumped it in a nearby large wastebasket. She should probably make sure the exam rooms were ready before patients came in.

Picking up her phone, she closed out the Bible app. Jessica had to be exaggerating. It couldn't be that bad.

Could it?

∾

The first week at the clinic raced by. Kathy began to find her rhythm in her job. The other woman in the office, a forty-something gal named Bev, managed scheduling and bills. Jessica doubled as the clinic's receptionist, checking in patients as they came in.

The front area was divided into two spaces: a comfortable waiting room with blue padded chairs and a television that showed a Tampa station, and the staff's working area. Jessica sat at the large U-shaped counter in front of a sliding glass window that allowed her to communicate with patients. Bev sat behind her across the room at the other end of the U, where there was another window that patients stopped at after they'd seen the doctor. Kathy had a space in between both women with her own computer and telephone.

Kathy helped the others when she could when she wasn't dealing with patients herself. She was grateful that she'd been trained out in Electronic Medical Records (EMR) – she carried a silver clinic laptop with her into each room and entered her findings into the system.

Dr. Gamble was in his fifties, with graying brown hair and a businesslike attitude. Patients liked him because he took the time to explain things to them. Kathy liked that he didn't constantly look over her shoulder but trusted her to get her job done.

She found herself relaxing a bit by Friday. Dr. Gamble certainly didn't strike her as an unreasonable man, though she never brought up what Jessica had told her. Jessica continued to treat her fairly and kindly. Bev was fun to go out to lunch with – she had a bit of sass to her and could make Kathy crack up with some of her stories.

Overall, it felt like a good situation. When Kathy used FaceTime to talk with her parents on Saturday, she emphasized the positives in her new living situation. Work was great, she told them and assured them she'd found a good congregation to worship with as well.

She didn't relay the conversation she'd had with Jessica on Monday. She figured it would only worry them and that was the last thing they needed.

The conversation weighed on her. She'd brought her lunch from home twice more that week, and had made sure she was alone in the office before opening her Bible app. It made her feel sneaky, but she wasn't trying to provoke a confrontation.

Sunday night she laid out her work clothes before going to bed. Before falling asleep she prayed as she always, adding the doctor and staff she worked with to her list. Her prayer was that somehow, they would see God through the way she acted.

Her prayers did not prepare her for the next day.

Kathy sat at her computer and brought up the next patient on the schedule. To her surprise, it was someone she knew. Mildred Higgins was a widow who attended services at the same church Kathy did. Mildred had been one of those to welcome her when she'd placed membership over a week ago. She'd insisted on taking Kathy out to lunch at a nearby Italian restaurant and been most kind with advice on where to shop for groceries and did she want a cat, because the Humane Society had them and was really wonderful?

Kathy had turned down the cat, but the lunch had helped drive back the little bit of loneliness she'd felt at being in a new town. Every time Kathy showed up to services Mildred was there to give her a hug and a hello as she leaned on her wooden cane.

Now, Kathy opened the door that led to the waiting room and spied Mildred sitting in one of the chairs, a large black pocketbook on her lap. "Mildred?"

Mildred's face lit up and she slowly got to her feet. She hobbled over to Kathy and said in a low voice, "I'm glad to see you."

Kathy gestured to the electronic scale that stood across from the door. Smiling, she said, "You might want to put your purse down – I bet it would add at least five pounds."

Mildred smiled but there was something about her that made Kathy think she was tense. After checking her weight, Kathy brought her into an exam room and waved her to a black plastic chair instead of the exam table. "How are you doing, Mildred?" she asked as she perched on a stool, placing her laptop on a nearby counter.

The older woman began to tremble. "Oh, Kathy, I've been so worried about this visit."

"Why?" Kathy asked. She glanced at the laptop – Mildred was there to discuss bloodwork she'd had done the week before.

"Well, I haven't been feeling quite right. Trouble sleeping, and sometimes very shaky," Mildred said. "I'm worried I've picked up some awful disease. My husband died of leukemia, and there's a history of cancer in my family."

Kathy could have accessed the lab results, but she knew it wasn't her place to discuss them with Mildred. Dr. Gamble had made it clear that unless he told her otherwise that was not her job. "Mildred, let me get your vitals, okay? I'm sure the doctor will let you know if something is wrong."

Kathy used a contact thermometer to get Mildred's temperature and clipped an O_2 sensor on one of her fingers for pulse and oxygen saturation. A quick check of Mildred's blood pressure showed it was higher than normal, but Kathy was certain it was because the poor woman was worried.

All other readings were normal, and Kathy recorded them on the laptop. "The doctor will be in soon," she said, standing.

"Kathy," Mildred reached out and touched her arm. "Could you please pray for me? Before you go? It would make me feel so much better."

Jessica's warnings sounded in Kathy's mind. But Mildred had been so kind to her. And a prayer could help her friend relax a bit and maybe bring down her blood pressure. "I would be happy to."

With Mildred's hands clasping hers, Kathy offered a short prayer asking God to be with Mildred and help her find peace whatever the doctor said. Mildred softly echoed Kathy's "Amen," and hugged her. "Thank you so much. I feel so much better."

Smiling, Kathy hugged her back. "Okay. I have to go now but I'll see you later."

Picking up her laptop she left the exam room. Kathy felt good about what had happened. She knew prayer was powerful and Mildred deserved the comfort it provided. And Mildred had initiated it, not Kathy. No one could possibly blame her for it.

At least, that's what she told the uneasy feeling in the pit of her stomach.

∾

Twenty minutes later, Kathy was in her space in the staff area checking her computer for the next scheduled patient when she heard Dr. Gamble call her name. Turning, she saw him standing in the doorway that led to his office, which was separated from the staff area by a narrow hallway.

He looked stern. "Ms. Abrams, I'd like to see you in my office."

Kathy felt her unease ramp up. She noticed Mildred talking to Bev, no doubt setting up her next appointment. The older woman looked a lot better than she had earlier, so Kathy suspected she'd gotten good news.

Standing, Kathy walked towards the doctor, who turned and entered his office. He waited for her to enter before shutting the door and saying, "Have a seat."

Gamble's office had three walls lined with bookcases that were filled to almost overflowing. His cherry desk took up a bit of space - there was barely room for two small leather chairs in front of it. Above the bookcases were a number of diplomas and citations.

Kathy sat in one of the leather chairs, her hands clasped together in her lap. The doctor took his own seat, a nice leather office chair, and steepled his hands together in front of him. He stared at her, frowning. "Ms. Abrams, Ms. Higgins informed me that you prayed with her today? During her exam?"

Oh, Mildred. Kathy suspected she'd meant well. A little frustrated, she asked, "Was Ms. Higgins complaining about it?"

The doctor's eyes narrowed. "On the contrary, she said she was quite grateful for the gesture. But that is not the point."

"Sir?"

"Ms. Abrams," Gamble said, "I am not permitted to pry into an applicant's personal views. However, to be honest, had I known you were a practicing Christian I would have thought twice about hiring you."

That sounded ominous. "Sir, have you had any reason to question my abilities before now?"

"No," Gamble admitted.

"And did Ms. Higgins tell you she requested that I pray with her?"

"That is irrelevant," Gamble said with a shake of his head. "This is a clinic, not a church, Ms. Abrams. You are not to discuss religion with our patients. Even if they bring it up. And you are certainly not to pray with them."

Kathy couldn't believe what she'd just heard. "Sir, does that not interfere with my personal rights?"

"We are not the government. This is a private practice, and I will run it as I see fit," Gamble said. "If you find the conditions here too difficult, you are welcome to seek other employment. I would be willing to give you a positive reference, despite your irrational beliefs."

Did he want to get rid of her? Because she was a Christian? Kathy thought that kind of thing happened in other countries, not the United States. She sat in front of Gamble stunned, not sure how to respond to Gamble's words.

After a moment of silence, Gamble said, "I hope we have an understanding, Ms. Abrams. Please return to your duties."

"Yes sir," she said, almost choking on the words. She got up and left the office, and once the door was shut behind her, she realized she was shaking.

Hoping not to be noticed by Bev or Jessica, Kathy headed for the break room. There was a small bathroom with a sink and toilet off the break room that was reserved for employees. Entering it, Kathy locked the door and ran water in the sink, trying to breathe normally and calm down.

She'd just been threatened with the loss of her job because she had prayed with a patient. She'd done what Jesus would have done and had been called on the carpet for it.

It was all well and good to be told to find another job. It wasn't that she probably couldn't land one – MAs were in demand, and she had no doubt Gamble would do as he said and give her a positive reference.

But did she want to? She'd just moved here. Kathy *liked* Sebring. She liked the clinic, current situation notwithstanding. Did she really want to possibly uproot her life again?

Gazing in the mirror, Kathy realized she was crying. She cupped cool water in her hands and splashed it over her hot face twice.

After a few moments she felt calm enough to go back out to the clinic. When she stepped out of the bathroom, she came face to face with Jessica. The office manager's expression was a combination of sternness and sympathy. "Are you all right?"

Nodding, Kathy said, "I'm fine."

"Good. Get back to work."

As Kathy passed her, Jessica added in a low voice, "I *did* warn you."

Kathy sighed. "I know," she said, and left the room.

Over the next two days, Kathy did her best to keep her head down and do her job. Fortunately, no other members of her congregation appeared in the clinic, and no other patient asked her to pray with them.

She noticed Jessica kept a closer eye on her than she had the first week. It made her nervous and she suspected they were looking for a reason to criticize her work. Kathy tried to ignore it – she knew nerves would lead to mistakes and at this point she couldn't afford to make any – but it added to her stress.

Gamble never mentioned the conversation they'd had on Monday. He remained polite with her but there was a coolness in their relationship now. Kathy decided to keep things as professional as possible. It was her only hope at this point.

She spent time praying about the situation and looking through the Bible, hoping for an idea of what to do. Two nights when she woke up at around two am, unable to fall back asleep, she prayed some more, asking what God's will was in this situation.

By the time she got off work on Wednesday, it was after five and Kathy was tired and stressed. Bible study started at seven pm, and she thought about skipping it. Part of her wanted to indulge in a footlong chili-cheese coney and a large Oreo cheesecake milkshake from Sonic and curl up on the couch surfing tv channels.

But she liked Bible study, and if she went ahead with her plans, it was almost as if the clinic was taking something else away from her. She didn't want that. Her Bible and notebook were already in her silver subcompact. If she hurried, she could still do Sonic and be on time for things.

Hoping the sugar in the shake would perk her up, she headed for the fast-food restaurant. She remembered something her mother would say when she or her brother would complain about going to Wednesday night Bible study:

"When you don't feel like going, it's because the Devil knows you really need it that night and tries to stop you."

Well, Mom, we'll see about that, she thought.

It was five minutes to seven when Kathy pulled into the parking lot of the Sebring Church of Christ. After pulling into a grassy portion of the lot, she grabbed her things and hurried into the well-lit brick building.

There were still a few people in the large foyer talking. Kathy noticed some boxes filled with baked goods on a padded oak pew to her right – the church had an active bread ministry, gathering day-old goods from some of the area grocery stores and distributing them to those with needs.

She stepped into the auditorium, which had a soaring high ceiling and many chandeliers to light the spacious room. No one was in front yet, so she had time to find a seat. But before she'd taken two steps, she heard someone say her name.

Mildred was sitting in the next to last pew on Kathy's right. She smiled and got to her feet. "Good evening, dear. How are you?"

Kathy gave her a quick hug. "I'm okay. Are you feeling better?"

Mildred cocked her head. "Yes, I am. But that 'okay' didn't sound very okay."

Eep. Mildred was perceptive. "It's just some stuff at work."

Mildred continued to stare at her, and Kathy suddenly found she was fighting tears. She was so tired and confused, and no one at work understood.

Seeing the change in Kathy, Mildred hugged her again. Speaking softly, she said, "Come sit with me. After Bible study you can take me out for a decaf coffee and we'll talk."

"I don't want to be a bother," Kathy sniffled.

"Hush. You're not a bother. Now, sit down, Carl is ready to start."

Stepping carefully past Mildred, Kathy sat next to her friend. She pulled out her notebook, ready to write down anything she'd need to remember from the announcements. Mildred smiled at her and patted her hand.

Well, Kathy had to admit it – her mom was right. Just sitting there with Mildred, knowing she wasn't alone, helped her feel better. And she'd almost stayed away.

Take that, Devil.

After Bible study, Kathy and Mildred met at a nearby Denny's. Tucked into a booth near the door, both women ordered decaf coffee. Kathy perused the menu but wasn't hungry, and Mildred said coffee was fine.

Once the server left to fetch their drinks, Mildred folded her hands on the table. "Now, what's wrong? I know you're far more upset than you're letting on."

Kathy stared at the table, wondering where to begin. "I got into trouble at work."

"But in what way?" Mildred asked. "You certainly seemed to know your job when I was there on Monday."

Kathy hated what she had to say next. "He found out I prayed with you." Swallowing, she looked up at Mildred, who appeared confused. "He's not a believer. In fact, he's quite hostile about it."

"Oh, for heaven's sake," Mildred said. "Did I cause this? I

thought he'd be pleased that you were so kind. I'm so sorry, Kathy."

"No, it's not your fault," Kathy said. The server appeared with their coffee and Kathy waited for her to leave before continuing. Adding some sugar to her coffee, she said, "He told me I can't discuss religion at work or pray with patients. And if I couldn't accept that I could find another job."

"But can he do that?" Mildred asked, pouring some cream in her coffee before offering it to Kathy. "Don't you have rights?"

Shrugging, Kathy poured a small amount of cream into her cup. "Apparently, because he's a private business, I don't have much recourse." Wrapping her hands around her cup, she said, "I don't know what to do. I don't want to move again – I like it here."

"You shouldn't have to move again," Mildred said. "This is so silly. There must be something we can do."

Concerned, Kathy said, "Mildred, please, don't do anything. I doubt it would help. I just...do I compromise? Am I betraying God if I do?"

"I don't believe so," Mildred said, sipping her coffee. "You don't have to pray with patients or discuss your religious beliefs while at work. But it certainly isn't fair."

"No, it's not," Kathy agreed. "I feel as if they're watching me, waiting for me to slip up so they can fire me. I don't know how to fix it, and I'm afraid."

"I'm sure you've been praying about it," Mildred said. "And I will add my prayers. Do your best job, Kathy. That's the key to getting through this. I know it must be hard, but God is on your side. Stay faithful, and it will work out in the end."

With a faint smile, Kathy said, "It helps just to talk about it, Mildred. I appreciate you listening to me."

"Oh, it's no bother," Mildred said. "I like you, Kathy. I hope the Lord will see fit to keep you in Sebring for a while.

"I hope so, too," Kathy said. "You are a joy to know, Mildred. I'm so glad we met."

The older woman blushed. "Now, don't say things like that, you'll embarrass me."

Kathy felt herself relax a bit. Just sharing her burden with Mildred had made it lighter. And she knew that the woman would indeed pray about the situation. Mildred was a precious friend, and Kathy prayed she could stay in Sebring with her for a while longer.

The next day, Kathy had just left an exam room when she nearly ran into Dr. Gamble. The man frowned when he saw her. "Ms. Abrams, please wait for me in my office."

Kathy felt her heart beat faster. She mentally ran over everything she'd done that morning – had she made a mistake in a chart? "Sir?"

"I believe you heard me," he snapped. She watched him go to the exam room next to the one she exited, take a deep breath, then go inside.

Her stomach churning, Kathy went into the office and sat down, placing her laptop on the seat beside her. She prayed silently, not knowing if she was about to lose her job. Gamble certainly appeared angry – but why?

Ten minutes later he marched into his office, shutting the door behind him. He sat in his chair and glared at her. "Ms. Abrams, are you aware that I've received no less than three phone calls this morning concerning you?"

"Sir?" she hadn't expected that. Had she offended a

patient? She couldn't imagine how. "What did these people say?"

He studied her a moment. "You really don't know anything about it?"

"No, sir," she said. "If I've offended someone and they've called to complain –"

"That's not what's going on," he said. "Have you been in contact with any of my patients recently outside of work?"

Uh-oh. "I spoke to Ms. Higgins last night."

He nodded. "I see. And you felt it necessary to share the conversation we had on Monday?"

"Ms. Higgins saw that I was upset," Kathy said. "I wasn't aware that our conversation was a secret, so yes, I told her about it."

Gamble pinched the bridge of his nose. "Do you realize the trouble you've caused the clinic?"

"Sir, what happened?" Kathy asked. Apparently, Mildred had done something, even after Kathy had asked her not to. Kathy wondered if in trying to help, Mildred had cost her her job.

"Ms. Higgins was quite indignant," Gamble said. "She told me that you had prayed with her at her request, and my forbidding it was ill-advised. She said that she would post a negative review of the clinic if my attitude persisted."

Panic rising in her, Kathy said, "Sir, I told her to do nothing. I didn't encourage anything like this."

"Yes, she mentioned that," Gamble said. "She also said she was contacting other patients of mine who shared her views. After her call two others – members of your congregation, I suspect – called to complain that they'd heard I discriminated against Christians, and if that were the case, they would find another doctor."

Kathy felt her heart sink. "Sir, I didn't want her or the

others to do anything like that. I'll talk to them, ask them to reconsider."

Gamble raised an eyebrow. "You'd do that? Even if they're on your side?"

"I have no desire to hurt the clinic," she replied. "I disagree with your rules, sir, but that doesn't mean I want any harm to you or your practice."

Gamble shook his head. "You are a strange woman, Ms. Abrams. I would think one of your intelligence wouldn't be taken in by religion."

Kathy chose her words carefully. "Many intelligent people believe in God and the Bible, sir. If I thought you were interested, I'd show you why. But I'm not going to force my beliefs on you."

Gamble drummed his fingers on his desk. "I won't lie to you – I'm tempted to fire you over this. Let those patients do what they want – I won't be blackmailed."

"I understand, sir," she replied, fighting to keep her voice level.

"However," he continued, "I must also take into consideration that you are a good worker, and you mesh well with the staff. And I really would rather not have this explode into some kind of religious war – it's likely a number of my patients believe in this nonsense and would take offense at my actions."

Kathy said nothing. She clasped her shaking hands together. *Your will, Lord. Let this be Your will.*

"I suggest a compromise," Gamble said. "I won't fire you. And if a patient *requests* prayer, you are free to participate with them. But you will not initiate such a request. Nor will you have religious discussions with patients you do not personally know. Will this satisfy you and your people?"

Kathy considered it. "It satisfies me, sir. I will let the others know that."

"Good," he said rising. "As long as you maintain your high quality of work, there should be no issues. But do not take my kindness as something to take advantage of. If I discover you're harassing patients with your beliefs I *will* fire you."

Kathy stood. "You don't have to worry about that, sir."

"All right. Now, let's get back to work," Gamble said, opening the door of his office.

Kathy went to her space in the staff area, relief almost making her dizzy. She would have to thank Mildred and the others for going to bat for her.

And of course, she needed to thank God. His hand had surely been at work in the situation.

Jessica came over to her. "Everything okay?" she asked.

Kathy smiled at her. "Everything is fine, thank you."

After hesitating a moment, Jessica lowered her voice. "I know about the phone calls. You're not fired?"

Kathy shook her head. 'No. Like I said, everything is fine."

Jessica stared at her. "Wow. Care to tell me and Bev about it over lunch at Olive Garden?"

Kathy considered it. It could be an opportunity to open a door with Jessica or Bev. If nothing else, it would build relationships that might someday give her a chance to share the gospel with those two women.

Smiling, she said, "That sounds great."

Thank You, God.

THE SIZE OF GRACE

Sarah slowed her steps as she noticed the figure standing in front of her second-floor apartment door. A male, she thought, but he was turned away so she couldn't see his face.

It was dark, with a clear sky showing a half moon and stars. Despite the pleasant temperatures this February evening in Tampa, no one else was outside of the apartment complex. The neighborhood was supposed to be safe, but Sarah's life had taught her to be wary.

Holding her Bible and notebook close to her chest, she fumbled in her handbag for the pepper spray she carried, nearly dropping her keys in the process. Once she had the spray in her hand, she climbed the steps as quietly as she could, hating that going up them hid the man from view.

As she approached her door, the man turned around. The yellowish light above her door showed her the jowls and small dark eyes of a man she'd rather forget. Sarah took a few steps back, putting some more distance between them. "Gary."

He smiled unpleasantly, showing his crooked tobacco-stained teeth. "Sarah. It's been a while. I had to get your old place to give me your forwarding address."

She tensed. "They shouldn't have given it to you. Please leave."

"Now, is that any way to treat an old employer?" he asked. "I need to talk to you."

She tightened her grip on the pepper spray. "I would rather not speak with you. As I told you last year, we're done."

"So you said," he nodded. "But really, Sarah, I'm going to talk to you, either in your apartment or out here. And this isn't the kind of thing you want your neighbors to hear."

She ground her teeth in frustration. He was larger than she was, and stronger. He hadn't made any threatening moves towards her that would justify the pepper spray, though she longed to use it.

A breeze caused the branch of a nearby oak tree to hit the wall, causing her to jump. A television played something faintly in a nearby apartment. Closer, she caught the aroma of frying beef as someone fixed a late dinner. Gary leaned against the metal railing that separated the walkway from the parking lot below, looking prepared to wait her out.

She tried once more to reason with him. "Gary, can't you leave me alone?"

"Sarah, why you gotta make this hard?" He held his hands up in a defensive gesture. "I promise, I'll be a gentleman."

She prayed. *Lord, protect me from this man.* She knelt down and put her Bible and notebook on the concrete. Standing, she pulled out her phone as she warned, "Don't come any closer. If you do, I'll use this pepper spray and call the police."

"So unfriendly," Gary said, shaking his head. He

remained a few feet in front of her, hands in the pockets of his jeans. "Not at all like Red Rose."

One hand went to her hair, held back by a black clip. "That's not me anymore."

"It can be," Gary said. "My actress got busted for drug possession. I need someone quick. Your film still sells after two years, did you know that?"

Her cheeks grew hot. "I'm not starring in any more of your films. Once was plenty."

He blew out a frustrated breath. "Is it because of Mitch? I know he could be a little rough, but it worked for the movie. I'm using another guy for this film. He's gonna be gentle, I promise."

Unbidden, memories of filming that one porn movie flooded her brain. It had been a difficult time in her life, and she'd needed rent money. A "friend" had introduced her to Gary, and she'd agreed to star in his latest, "Red Rose Does It With Style." Gary had been tickled that she was a natural redhead and even had some acting experience from her days in community theater.

The filming had been a degrading experience. Gary kept saying they were creating "art" but to her it felt like something dirty. She never felt she was respected – not by Gary, who openly leered at her when she was unclothed, or Mitch, whose idea of passion left bruises on her arms.

She shook her head as she shoved the memories into a mental box. "I can't do it, Gary. If that's what you wanted to talk about, we're done here."

"I don't get it. Did you get religion or something?" he asked.

She swallowed. "Yes," she said. "As you put it, I 'got' religion."

"Hmmm," he said. His gaze went to her Bible on the ground nearby. "Well, that's interesting."

His tone made her nervous. "Gary, I need you to leave."

"Hold on," he said. "If you won't act for me, you could back my latest film. Say, to the tune of five grand?"

Her mouth dropped open. "You can't be serious."

"I sure am," he said. He glanced around the complex. "This ain't a bad place. You got some money, right?"

"I don't have $5,000," Sarah replied, "and if I did, I wouldn't give it to you. Now, leave me alone."

"Now hold up," he said, raising a hand. "You go to church now, right? Do those good people know about Red Rose?"

She froze, her stomach churning. She wanted to tell him to leave again, but she couldn't get words past the tightening of her throat.

"I thought so," Gary said with a nod. "It would be a shame, wouldn't it, if they found out? Christians aren't into my kind of art, you know. They can be downright unforgiving."

She thought of Dan Biggs, the preacher of her congregation, and Ashley, her friend who taught her the truth. They didn't even know – she couldn't work up the courage to tell them.

How would they react? How would the church react? Sarah thought of a couple of the older couples, who seemed so stiff and stern. She could see their lips curling, condemnation in their eyes.

Her voice came back. She held up her phone. "I'm dialing the police on the count of three. Leave. One…"

Gary held up a placating hand. "I'm going, I'm going. Think about it, Sarah. I will do what I say, you know that about me." Turning and walking off, he spoke over his shoulder. "I'll be in touch."

She watched as he got to the end of the walkway and turned left, out of sight. With a cry she snatched up her books and unlocked the door to her apartment, darting inside. After locking the door and shooting the deadbolt, she leaned against the door. Dropping her things, she sank to the floor and wept.

Sarah stared at her computer screen, not actually seeing the playlist she was supposed to be putting together for the local talk radio station. Her mind kept running back to the previous evening. Gary's sneering face and his threatening words had robbed her of sleep the night before and she felt dull and out of touch.

"Hello?" A slender hand waved in front of Sarah's screen. "Earth to Sarah, Earth to Sarah."

She blinked and turned towards the speaker. Ashley was standing next to her desk, her blue eyes bright with curiosity. "You okay? You looked like you were spacing out."

"Um," Sarah mumbled, blinking a couple of times and trying to stifle a yawn. "I had a hard time sleeping last night."

The office the two women shared held two desks, several filing cabinets, and a set of shelves that held thick binders filled with information about the station, their advertisers, and the like. A window behind the desks looked out to the parking lot of the strip mall they operated out of.

Ashley squinted at Sarah's screen. "You've got Parson's Florist Shop twice in a row," she said. "You know how Carl gets when that happens."

With a cluck of her tongue Sarah deleted one of the spots. "Thanks for catching that." Carl was one of the morning hosts and got very cranky when they messed up his ads.

Ashley cocked her head. "You've been acting weird all morning. Is everything all right?"

Sarah bit her lip. Ashley was twenty-five, two years older than Sarah, married going on three years. She'd taken Sarah under her wing when Sarah started working at the station and helped her stay on the straight and narrow. She also taught her about Jesus and stood with her when she was baptized.

Ashley, who Sarah had never heard utter anything stronger than, "Oh, shoot." Who went shopping with Sarah for clothes for worship services and even bought her a dress she'd admired. Who was bright and cheerful and seemingly untouched by darkness.

Before Sarah could stop herself, she was crying.

"Hey, hey," Ashley said, patting her shoulder. Glancing towards the halfway open door to their office, she said, "Just a sec," and closed it. Once that was done, she pulled her padded office chair closer to Sarah and sat. Before Sarah knew it, she was pulled into a reassuring hug. "It's okay. Whatever it is, it'll be okay."

Sarah shook her head. "Not this," she sobbed. "I'm a bad person, Ashley."

Her friend stroked her head. "I don't believe that. You're a child of God, and He loves you."

Sarah wanted to believe her friend. But the weight of her past was heavy on her soul. "I need to talk to you. But not here. And maybe Dan, too."

Ashley gave her a final squeeze before letting her go. "All right. After work okay? I'll see if Dan is free."

Sarah wiped her eyes. "What about Roger? Do you guys have plans tonight?"

"Is this important?" Ashley asked.

Sarah swallowed. "Yeah. It...it's a problem."

Ashley pulled out her phone. "Roger will understand. There's stuff in the fridge he can nuke for dinner if he gets hungry. I'll see if Dan is able to meet with us. His place?"

Sarah thought of Dan's family, his wife Marcia and their two children. "Maybe...the church building?"

"Okay, no problem," Ashley said, her thumbs flying over her iPhone's screen.

Sarah watched her friend sadly, wondering if they would still be friends after her revelation.

Dan Biggs was in his mid-thirties, with thinning brown hair and a calm manner to him. Unlocking the door to his office, he gestured Sarah and Ashley to enter. "It's a bit of a mess," he apologized, moving two trash bags filled with donated clothing from a dark red leather couch. "Either of you want some water?"

"Yes, thank you," Sarah said, sitting on the sofa. Ashley sat beside her while Dan got three bottles of water from a mini fridge behind his metal desk. After handing one each to Sarah and Ashley, he settled across from them in a gray recliner that had seen better days. "So, Sarah, Ashley said there's a problem of some kind you need help with?"

"Sort of," Sarah said, turning the plastic bottle in her hands. She took a deep breath, praying she could do this. "The thing is...I haven't been totally honest with either of you."

She stole a glance at Dan, who cocked his head. "How so?"

She shifted in her seat. "There's something in my past...I didn't want to say anything, I was afraid, but it might come out now and I don't know what to do."

Ashley looked nervous. "What is it? Are the police looking for you?"

"No," Sarah snapped, then felt guilty. "No...it's not like that."

Dan leaned forward. "You know, I think before you say another word we need to pray about this. You're obviously upset and afraid, but you know there's no sin that God can't forgive."

"What about people?" Sarah asked. "Some things people won't forgive."

Dan put his bottle on the floor. "Let's pray. Okay?"

Sarah bowed her head as Dan led them in prayer. He asked for courage for Sarah and understanding for himself and Ashley. He thanked God for His love and the sacrifice of His Son, ending with, "In Jesus' name, amen."

After the prayer Sarah opened her bottle and took a drink. Not looking at Dan or Ashley, she talked about living in the wrong area of Tampa, having trouble finding a job and suddenly needing rent money.

"Someone at the apartment complex knew a man who made films. And he happened to need an actress right away and would pay enough to cover my rent and then some." Her eyes filled with tears. "I was desperate. My mom had kicked me out when I turned 18, I had no one to help me..."

Dan's voice was soft. "What kind of films, Sarah?"

She shuddered. "Pornographic."

She heard Ashley's sharp intake of breath and winced.

She kept her gaze glued to the water bottle in her hands, afraid of what she'd see in her friend's eyes.

The silence hung heavy for a moment. Then Dan said, "Sarah, are you sorry for it?"

She jerked her head in a nod.

"And are you still making such films?"

"No," she whispered. "It was just the one. I swear."

"Sarah," Dan said, "Look at me."

She shook her head. She was trembling, afraid of what was going to happen.

Dan's voice was gentle. "Sarah. I won't lie: I'm shocked. And I wish you had been able to tell me before this. But it doesn't change the fact that Jesus died for all your sins. Including that one. He forgave you; how could I do any less?"

She lifted her head. Dan looked solemn as he leaned forward, resting his elbows on his knees. But he didn't look like he thought she was trash.

"Ashley..." she stammered. Her friend hadn't said anything. "I'm sorry. I should have told you sooner. Please don't hate me."

Ashley grabbed one of her hands. "I don't hate you. I'm... it's weird and a little disturbing. But that's not who you are now, Sarah. I *know* that."

Sarah squeezed her hand. "Are we still friends?"

Ashley let go of her hand to put her arms around her. "Yes. I'm glad you finally told me. This must have been eating at you big time."

"Sarah," Dan said, "You said something about this coming out. Why?"

Hugging herself, she told Ashely and Dan about Gary and his visit the previous evening. "He said he'd reveal it to the congregation. But I don't have that kind of money unless I borrow it."

"Call the police," Ashley said. "Blackmailing is illegal, they can arrest him."

"It's not that simple," Dan said. "It will come down to a 'he said/she said' situation. And if the police get involved it will definitely come out."

"People will hate me," Sarah said. "Right?"

"Most people won't," Ashley argued.

"Some would have a problem with it, yes," Dan said. "But Sarah, that is *their* problem, not yours. I think you underestimate people here."

Her eyes filled with tears. "Do they have to know?"

Dan looked thoughtful. "I can understand why you don't want it revealed, but it takes away his hold on you if you do."

"What if he decides to tell my boss?" Sarah said, suddenly feeling ill.

"Don't worry about Sean," Ashley said. "He's not a Christian, but he's a big believer in second chances."

"What do you want to do, Sarah?" Dan asked. "We can make an announcement on Sunday morning. I'll help."

She thought about it. "I – I don't know. If most people turn their backs on me, where will I go? It's such a risk."

Dan sighed. "I'm not going to force you, but this Gary fellow might. You need to take that into account. If it's going to come out, it's better if you control it."

"Maybe I should take out a loan..." Sarah started but stopped when Dan shook his head.

"Don't pay him. You do that once, he'll be back. He'll drain you dry, Sarah."

She sighed, knowing he was right. "I'll think about it."

"Okay," Dan said. "Let's pray again before we leave."

Sarah bowed her head as Dan asked God for grace,

forgiveness, and wisdom. Misery threatened to overwhelm her. She thought she'd feel better confiding in Dan and Ashley, but now she was wondering if it had been a mistake.

After Dan finished Sarah got to her feet. "Thank you," she said. "for not looking down on me."

"I'll never look down on you, Sarah," Dan said. "No matter what."

Ashley stood and touched Sarah's arm. "Listen. Why don't we go grab a bite to eat at Olive Garden?"

Sarah looked at Ashley uneasily. "You don't have to go anywhere with me, Ashley. It's okay."

"No, it's not," Ashley said. "Look, Dan's right. You're a child of God just like I am. And you're my friend. What kind of friend would I be if I ditched you? Please come have dinner with me."

A glimmer of hope sparked in Sarah's dark mood. "Okay...but only if Roger is okay with it."

"He will be," Ashley said. "Let me call him."

As her friend contacted her husband, Sarah wondered what would happen after tonight. If Gary would only leave her alone!

She soon learned that was not the case.

The Sunday morning sky was filled with clouds, and as Sarah found a space in the church building's parking lot, she debated bringing an umbrella into the auditorium. Unsure if she had one in her car, she parked and twisted towards the backseat, seeing if one was there.

A knock on her window got her attention, and to her dismay she saw Gary leering at her. He was dressed in a dark blue business suit with a black tie. "Hey," he called through the window.

Frightened and angry, she turned the car back on so she could lower her window. "What are you doing here?"

He gave her an innocent look. "I wanted to talk to you. I saw you leave this morning and just followed along." He looked over his shoulder at the brick building that the congregation worshipped in. "Looks like a nice place."

Rolling up her window, Sarah turned off the car and grabbed her things. Stepping out, she said, "I am not talking to you here. Go away."

"You're going to turn away a sinner?" Gary's tone was mocking. "No, I think I'll hang around. Might even give some testimony."

She felt a chill sweep over her. "Gary, please don't."

He gave her a mean smile. "Well, Red Rose, that depends on you. Shall we?"

Sarah walked to the building, Gary next to her. She tried to think, but her brain felt as if a fog had descended on it. She saw fellow believers who called out greetings and she managed to nod in response, praying her fear didn't show.

One of the older men, a retired teacher by the name of Harry, held open the door for Sarah and Gary. "Good morning," he smiled.

"Good morning," Gary replied. "Nice to be here."

Sarah murmured a greeting and kept walking, hoping Gary would not stop to converse. Thankfully, he fell into step behind her.

They were about five minutes early, the large foyer filled with people dressed nicely, chatting with one another in a pleasant hum.

Dan Biggs was heading for the door. Thankful, Sarah stepped into his path. "Good morning, Dan."

He stopped, giving her a puzzled look. "Sarah? I'm heading to the teen class, can I talk to you afterwards?"

Gary stepped forward. "Hi. I'm Gary Finch. I'm a former employer of Sarah's."

Sarah saw understanding flash in Dan's eyes. "I'm Dan Biggs, the preacher here," he said, shaking Gary's hand. "I don't believe you've visited us before."

Smiling, Gary said, "No, I needed to talk to Sarah about some business, and discovered she was here. Glad to meet all these wonderful people."

"I'm certain," Dan said. Turning to Sarah, he asked, "Have you considered what we talked about the other night?"

She knew what he meant. A glance at Gary's smirking face made only one decision possible. Praying she wasn't ruining her life she said, "I think we should deal with it."

"We will," Dan promised. Glancing at his watch, he said, "I need to go teach my class. Hope you enjoy our Bible Study, Mr. Finch."

Sarah held her breath as Dan left. She hoped Gary wouldn't question her about the conversation. "We should find a seat."

Gary put a hand on her arm. "I'm going to need an answer soon, Sarah. I'll give you an hour to think it over."

"Gary, there's a worship service after the Bible Study," Sarah said. "Can't it wait until after that?"

He frowned. "Hour and a half. Then I stand up and make an announcement."

Her heart hammering, she pulled away from him and entered the auditorium. Picking a pew near the back, she slid onto the dark blue padded seating. Gary sat next to her and leaned back, folding his arms over his chest.

Sarah didn't know what to do. There was no way to warn

Dan before service, and Gary might well disrupt things before the preacher knew what was going on. She didn't dare text him with Gary sitting right next to her.

Desperately, she prayed that something could be done. Even if she didn't know what it could be.

The five-minute bell had sounded, indicating Bible Study was almost done. Sarah had tried to concentrate on the lesson Harry was teaching on Proverbs, but she couldn't keep focused. Gary sat silently next to her, appearing relaxed but alert.

Dan walked into the auditorium, followed by Ashley and the teen class. Ashley spotted Sarah and immediately headed for her pew, sitting next to her while the teens found places to sit in the half empty auditorium. Dan walked to the podium and spoke quietly to Harry, who nodded and said, "Dan has an announcement to make."

Sarah was puzzled. Ashley usually taught first and second grade during Bible Study – what was she doing here? Before she could ask, Dan spoke.

"We're doing things a little differently this morning. I've asked that the children remain in their classes for now, while I make this announcement." Dan shot a glance at Sarah, who nodded slightly. She braced herself.

"Before I make my announcement, I want to share something from God's word," Dan said. "Please turn to John, chapter eight, beginning in verse one."

Sarah tried not to react, but the account in John eight was one she knew very well. She noticed other members looking at each other, puzzled as they flipped pages in their Bibles.

Dan continued, "You're no doubt familiar with this account from the life of Jesus – it's about the woman caught in adultery. Pharisees brought her to Jesus, asking Him if she should be stoned according to the law."

Gary appeared bored, and Sarah hoped he stayed that way. He obviously didn't know the story, but he was about to get an education.

"Jesus told them, 'Let he who is without sin cast the first stone,'" Dan said. "His words condemned her accusers, and they all left, leaving her alone with the Lord. He asked if there was anyone left to condemn her, and she answered, 'No one, Lord.' He then told her to go and sin no more."

A line appeared between Gary's eyes. Sarah felt worry stab at her. Would Gary interrupt?

"You may wonder why I tell you this," Dan said. "This woman was held in contempt for her sin, and let's make no mistake, what she did was wrong. However, instead of treating her badly, our Lord offered compassion and a chance to make her life right."

Gary turned to her, his eyes narrowing. "What's going on?" he said in a harsh whisper.

Sarah shook her head, looking over at Dan. Ashley took one of her hands and squeezed it reassuringly.

Gary frowned, leaning forward a bit as Dan continued.

"But what would we have done with her? I ask you this because a sister came to me earlier this week to confess a sin from her past. A sin she has repented of. But one she fears will cause her brothers and sisters to turn away from her in disgust and shame."

"Just a minute!" Gary shouted, coming to his feet. Sarah nearly fainted. Everyone was looking at Gary – and at her.

"Sir," Dan said calmly, "please sit down." The preacher glanced at a man sitting near the front of the room, a man

Sarah recognized as a county sheriff. The sheriff got up and headed towards Gary with an intimidating expression.

Gary glared at the man but slowly sat back down. The sheriff took a seat in a pew across from Gary and kept an eye on him.

"This man," Dan said, "thinks you will treat this sister badly. Because she starred in a pornographic movie he produced. Now he threatens her, telling her you won't accept her as your erring sister who is trying to do what is right."

Taking the mike from its stand, Dan stepped from behind the podium and walked to where the first pew was. "Sarah, will you come forward?"

Gary shook his head. But Sarah slipped past Ashley and walked towards Dan, feeling everyone's eyes on her, knowing her face must be beet red.

When she got to Dan, the preacher put an arm around her shoulders. "Sarah, have you repented of your sin?"

She looked at Dan, her eyes filling with tears. "Yes," she said into the mike her held out.

"God bless you, sister. I love you," Dan said, hugging her. Turning to the congregation, Dan said, "Who will show our sister the love of Christ?"

He'd hardly finished speaking before Ashley was leaving her pew. But she wasn't the first to reach Sarah. To her shock, she saw pews begin to empty as men and women stepped up to her, offering her hugs, telling her they loved her, offering to pray for her.

To be sure, there were several members who sat, arms folded, frowns on their faces when she caught their gaze. But they were outnumbered by the members who came up to her.

Harry's wife Brenda, her gray hair in a tidy bun, took

Sarah's face in her hands. "That took a lot of courage to admit, dear. I'm proud of you for wanting to make things right."

"I..." Sarah stammered. She didn't know what to say to Brenda – or anyone else, for that matter. "Thank you" hardly seemed to cover it.

Pulling her close, Brenda whispered in Sarah's ear. "We all have things to be ashamed over. Praise God for His grace."

Sarah blinked back tears. "Thank you."

In her fear, she'd forgotten about the size of God's grace. And that it covered not only everyone else's sins, but hers as well.

She couldn't stop crying. How could she have doubted these wonderful people?

Ashley handed her a tissue with a grin. "God is good."

"Yes," Sarah said. She glanced at where she'd been sitting and found herself staring at an empty pew.

Gary had gone, his threat robbed of its power. Sarah felt a relief so profound her legs shook.

Dan was still standing nearby. She turned and gave him a hug, grateful to him and Ashley for loving her, despite knowing the worst. And thankful that they were right – love had won the day.

Yes, God was good.

THE ROAD FROM HELL

Megan heard the paper in her trembling hands rattle in the quiet of the courtroom. Before she'd entered this nightmare, she'd never been in a courtroom, only catching glimpses of them on shows such as "Law and Order."

Even though she stood in front of the judge's bench now, the details of the room swam in her vision. Dark cherry wood dominated, from the jury box to her left with its chairs padded in powder blue to the sea of benches behind a rail of the same wood – benches that held a number of her, and most importantly, Anna's friends.

Then there were the two long tables in front of the rail, their polished surfaces gleaming under the fluorescent lights. On the left, Carla Wells, the District Attorney who'd kept her and Ed apprised of the proceedings in the case over the past long two months. And, on the right...

On the right sat the reason she was here. The reason for her nightmare. A young man, twenty-four years old according to what she'd read. His light brown hair was neatly combed and he wore a blue blazer and a white shirt with a gray tie and matching gray trousers.

Patrick James Morrison. The murderer of her only child.

Sitting next to Morrison was his attorney, a man Megan loathed. His black hair was graying at his temples and he looked unconcerned as he waited for her to speak, his wire rim glasses winking in the lights overhead.

Megan took a deep breath. Her eyes searched the crowd behind the prosecutor's table and met Ed's. Her husband sat in the first row. Dark shadows marred his eyes and she could see the tears standing in them as he met her gaze. But he still managed to give her a nod of encouragement.

She blinked back her own tears. She'd vowed she wouldn't give Morrison the satisfaction of breaking down during her statement. She would get through this. For Anna's sake.

Glancing down at the paper in her hands, its whiteness a startling contrast to the cheap dark blue carpet she stood on, Megan began to speak.

"Twenty years ago, my husband and I were given an answer to our prayers. A beautiful baby girl we named Anna Marie. From the time I held her in my arms she – she brought me so much joy..."

Megan swallowed, tasting her tears. Memories flitted through her mind: Anna at five, helping Megan bake gingerbread for the first time. Anna at thirteen, sitting with Megan in the emergency room with a broken arm thanks to a fall from the sturdy oak tree in their front yard. Anna at eighteen, radiant in her navy cap and gown the day she graduated from high school.

Blinking hard she refocused on the statement she'd labored on so hard ever since the district attorney had told her she would be allowed to make a victim impact statement. *Keep it together*, she thought. *Just a few minutes...*

"Growing up, she loved to dance. She learned tap and performed at her high school talent show – she was so good. She wanted to become a teacher but was hoping she'd always be able to dance."

Another swallow. The paper creased as she gripped it tighter. "Anna also loved animals and spent time working at the county shelter. The other people who work there tell me she was one of the kindest persons they'd ever met. The animals loved her and so did just about everyone who knew her."

No matter how hard she tried, she couldn't keep her voice from breaking as she continued. "Two months ago, you stole that sweet special girl from us because you didn't care enough to pay attention to what you were doing. Replying to a text was more important to you than driving safely. And my poor daughter paid for your carelessness with her life!"

Now she raised her eyes from the paper she held and glared at Morrison. "Thanks to you I will never see my – my daughter graduate from college, never see her walk down the aisle to be married, never hold her firstborn. And nothing you do or say can ever change that."

She paused, clenching her jaw against the sob that rose in her throat. A couple of people in the audience were crying softly. Morrison met her gaze for a few seconds before dropping his head. She couldn't see his face, but his shoulders shook.

White hot rage flooded her. Was he laughing at her? Mocking her pain? His lawyer put a hand on Morrison's back as if to calm him. There was no one to calm Megan, though. She lowered the paper she'd clutched like a lifeline and stared at the monster before her.

"One day," she said, hearing venom in her voice and not caring, "God will judge you for what you've done to us. And I pray he sends you to Hell where you belong."

With that, she turned away from Morrison and his attorney and walked to where Ed was sitting. She could hear people murmuring to each other, but she ignored everyone but her husband.

As she sank onto the hard bench beside Ed, he looked at her, a little puzzled. "I don't remember that last comment being part of your statement," he whispered.

Megan realized she was shaking. She didn't bother replying to her husband. Instead she dug in her purse for a tissue, the tears back now that she was done speaking. As she wiped her damp cheeks and blew her nose the judge, a thin man with curly brown hair and glasses banged his gavel and asked, "Would anyone else like to make a victim impact statement?"

The murmurs evaporated. Megan felt the tissue she held shred in her hands as she waited. Wells had told her that no one else was scheduled to speak besides Megan, but she'd wondered if any of her friends would change their minds.

But there was one statement she was waiting for. Her gaze zeroed in on the back of Morrison's head. What would this murderer possibly have to say for himself? How would he excuse what he'd done? He hadn't bothered to deny it, pleading guilty to vehicular manslaughter.

And because he'd done that, he would only serve ten years in jail. Megan's jaw clenched in anger. Only half the time her daughter had been permitted to live on the earth. It wasn't fair. But the district attorney told her the deal was for the best, that it saved Anna's family the agony of a trial.

Megan blinked. Morrison was getting to his feet. The judge must have asked him if he had a statement while she'd been lost in thought.

The man who'd taken her daughter's life hesitated a few seconds, then looked back over his shoulder. Megan was shocked to see tears staining his face. Tears? Was it possible that when she thought he'd been laughing at her he was actually weeping?

Megan frowned and shook her head. It had to be an act. *Had* to be. She couldn't believe this piece of trash could feel any pain, much less hers.

Morrison's gaze paused on her for a brief second, then he turned back to face the judge. When he spoke, his voice was hoarse and choked.

"I know whatever I say here can never make up for what happened that night. I – I wasn't thinking, I was just letting my roommate know I'd be home soon. I just took my eyes off the road for a couple of seconds…"

He gulped and Megan saw a shudder go through his body. Her hands clenched into fists as she fought to keep from screaming at Morrison. She felt Ed's hand, slightly damp, covering hers, trying to calm her.

"I know I d-deserve my sentence. I just wish…I wish it hadn't happened. That I'd seen her in time. I wish I could… could make it all right."

He turned back towards Megan and she saw fresh tears streaming down his face. "Mr. and Mrs. Stanton, I'm so sorry. Please, please, forgive me. Forgive –"

It was more than she could take. Before she realized it Megan was on her feet, her words almost incomprehensible as she snarled, "*How dare you!*"

She felt Ed's hand on her arm, tugging at her, trying to get her to sit down. People were talking around her, the judge was hammering his gavel and saying something about her controlling herself. But all she could focus on was Morrison's white face.

His pale blue eyes were wide as she glared at him, pouring all the tears she'd wept and all the hate she'd nursed into her stare.

His mouth moved, but nothing came out. Megan noticed with contempt that his nose was running, snot mixing with his tears. He looked utterly pathetic as he shook and wept, one hand outstretched towards her.

Megan felt gladness blooming at the sight. It was only right that he suffer for what he'd done. She prayed he would suffer far, far worse in the days and weeks to come...

Morrison's attorney was standing next to him, his hand on his shoulder, talking softly into his ear. He finally tore his gaze from Megan and, nodding, turned back to face the judge.

Love your enemies.

The Bible verse came unbidden into her mind and was like a bucket of cold water. Love *this* man? That couldn't be what the Bible meant! How could she feel anything but hatred for the person who had taken her precious daughter away from her?

"Mrs. Stanton!"

Megan blinked. The judge eyed her from his perch in front of the courtroom. His tone was firm. "Please take your seat and remain silent or I will have to ask you to leave."

Carla Wells was leaning over the rail, her voice quiet but urgent. "Megan, please sit down. This won't help matters."

Stunned, Megan let Ed pull her back onto the bench. She glanced around and saw some strangers on the other side of the room – the defense's side, she thought – giving her stern looks before turning back to face the front of the courtroom. Her cheeks warmed as she realized how her outburst must have appeared.

One woman who sat behind the defense table stared at her a long moment as the room fell silent. She had curly brown hair that showed gray roots and she twisted the strap of a black shoulder bag as she gazed at Megan. Unlike the others, there was no disapproval in her expression – only sorrow and compassion.

Megan tore her gaze away from the stranger. She wanted nothing from Morrison's friends and family, least of all their pity.

The judge waited a moment, as if to see whether someone else would jump up and shout. Then he said, "You may continue Mr. Morrison."

The killer shook his head. "I – I guess I've said all I can say, sir."

The judge nodded. "Remain standing as I pronounce your sentence."

Megan only half heard the judge's stern speech to Morrison. She didn't care what His Honor had to say, unless he was going to throw out the plea deal and deliver a harsher sentence to the criminal. Now, she just wanted this ordeal to end so she could go home, away from this room of dark wood and cheap blue carpet. So she could try to put together her shattered life.

She closed her eyes and all she could see was her precious Anna. But now the images had to do with Anna as a child sitting with Megan with her illustrated Bible while Megan told her the story of Jesus loving the children. Anna, being baptized by Ed at age fourteen. Anna, sunburned but happy after a week at Bible camp...

Love your enemies.

I can't, she prayed, fighting a surge of anger at God. I can't love him. Don't ask me to.

"All rise!"

Megan's eyes flew open. The judge was standing, as were others around her. Megan scrambled to her feet. It was done. Whatever justice she could expect here on Earth had been given out.

Carla Wells leaned over the railing and embraced Megan. "I know how difficult this was for you," the district attorney said. "But it's over now. He's going to pay."

Megan looked over at Morrison's side of the room, where the woman with gray roots was weeping and hugging the killer. Megan's stomach twisted and she swallowed the bile that rose in her throat. "It's not enough," she muttered.

Carla pulled away, her hands resting on Megan's shoulders. "I know you wanted a harsher sentence, but believe me when I say this is all for the best. Anna can rest now."

Megan shook her head. She knew that arguing this was pointless. The sentence had been passed and nothing could change it.

Wells next hugged Ed, who said, "Thank you, Carla, for all you've done for us. For our family."

"It was my pleasure," Wells said. Her eyes narrowed as she looked behind Megan and her husband. "It looks like a reporter from the *Palmetto City Times* is trying to get over here. You don't have to talk to him, I'll handle it."

Megan turned to see a stout young man with bushy blond hair and a mustache working his way through the people in the aisle. He held a small spiral notebook in his hand. He caught Megan's gaze and called out, "Mrs. Stanton?"

One of Anna's friends came up to her and Ed and she tore her gaze from the blond man, hoping Carla could head him off. She focused on the slender girl in front of her, a member of Anna's dance class if she recalled correctly. She accepted the young woman's tearful embrace, willing herself not to flee the courthouse.

For several minutes she and Ed accepted condolences and congratulations from those who knew Anna or them. Megan was able to keep herself together until their preacher, Jack Peters came up to them.

Peters was a large man with thinning black hair and a beard. He hugged first Megan, then Ed and said, "I know how difficult this has been for the both of you. Maybe now you can find peace."

"Thanks, Jack," Ed said, his voice strained. "Please keep praying for us. This is so hard."

"I'm sure," Peters said. He took Megan's hand and hesitated, as if he were considering his words. "Megan, I'd be willing to talk to you sometime about your feelings in all this. You...you're clearly in a lot of pain right now."

She stiffened. "I lost my only child, Jack. How could I not be in pain?"

"I know," he said quickly. "It's just that...I'm concerned for you." He glanced around the emptying courtroom. "I only want to help."

Megan shook her head, unable to stop fresh tears. She suspected she knew what Peters wanted to talk about and she was having none of it. "You can't, Jack. You can't raise the dead and you can't get me justice in this life. I'm hoping and praying God will give it to me in the next."

She watched as the preacher folded his lips together as if to hold back the words he wanted to say. He gave her hand a final squeeze. "I'll pray for you. Both of you."

Nodding, Megan wiped her face. "Thank you. Ed, please take me home."

Peters stepped aside so they could make their way to the aisle. Megan had one foot on just started for the door when a voice behind her called, "Mr. and Mrs. Stanton! Please, just a moment!"

Megan would have kept walking, but Ed stopped and turned. She saw her husband frown and looked over her shoulder. The blond reporter stood several feet behind them, pen poised above his notepad. Behind him, Carla Wells glowered.

The reporter took a step forward. "Alan Baker, *Palmetto City Times*. I just have a couple of questions..."

Ed shook his head. "We're not talking to the press. I'm sorry." He turned back and took Megan's arm. She leaned on him, grateful.

Baker wasn't so easily dissuaded. "Mrs. Stanton, did you mean what you said? You want Patrick Morrison to burn in Hell?"

Megan tightened her grip on her husband's arm. She clenched her teeth to keep hot words from spilling out. She saw Peters step past her, presumably to head the reporter off. She prayed he was successful.

"Mrs. Stanton!" Baker raised his voice. Behind her she heard Peters speaking in low tones, maybe telling him to lay off. If that's what he was doing the reporter wasn't listening. "Mrs. Stanton! Aren't you a Christian? Doesn't your faith demand you forgive Patrick Morrison?"

Love your enemies.

She felt herself stop, the doors out of this horrible room just out of reach. She turned to see the reporter staring at her, an eyebrow raised, ready to write whatever words she might utter.

She felt a surge of hatred for the man, for his questions, his presumption. She felt Ed put his arm around her, trying to get her to turn back to the doors. She resisted. She wanted to rail at Baker, ask him if he'd ever lost a child, ask him how he could tell her what her faith demanded.

Before she could open her mouth, Peters placed himself between her and the reporter. "Look," the preacher said to Baker, his voice pleasant but firm, "this family has been through an ordeal. Have the decency to give them some privacy to cope."

"Come on, Megan," Ed urged, once again trying to turn her away. This time she allowed him to, while Baker began to pepper Peters with questions. She felt badly about Jack now having to deal with Baker but the preacher chose to step in.

Even as Ed guided her through the large wooden doors to the hallway outside with its marble floor causing their footsteps to echo off the white walls she still heard Baker's challenging question: *Doesn't your faith demand you forgive Patrick Morrison?*

I can't, she thought stubbornly, her gaze on the floor so she wouldn't have to make eye contact with anyone and maybe have to converse with them. I'm sorry, God. I can't. I *won't*.

The next morning Megan was surprised to find Ed up before her. Normally he wandered into their small kitchen after she was already halfway through her first cup of coffee. Yet when she opened her eyes she found herself alone in bed.

After a quick trip to the bathroom Megan threw on a pair of jeans and an old stained pink t-shirt she wore around the house. Sliding slippers on her feet, she headed for the kitchen where she found Ed sitting in the breakfast nook poking at a toasted frozen waffle he'd topped with butter and syrup.

"You're up early," she commented, heading for the coffeepot. She hadn't slept well and couldn't wait for the caffeine jolt.

Ed looked up, startled. "Yeah. Well...I couldn't sleep."

"I know what you mean," Megan said as she poured herself a cup of coffee. She added artificial sweetener (in her mind she heard Anna saying "Yuck!" and had to swallow a lump in her throat) and hazelnut creamer that Ed apparently had pulled out of the refrigerator.

"Let me get some of this in me and I'll get the paper," Megan said as she inhaled the restoring fragrance of her drink.

Ed shifted in his wooden ladder-back chair – one of four the three of them had found at a Goodwill store and restored over a long weekend. "Uh, don't bother. I – I got it already."

Megan looked at the small square oak table where Ed sat and saw no sign of the *Palmetto City Times*. "Where is it?"

Her husband took a deep breath. "I threw it away."

"What?" Megan frowned. "Why?"

"Sweetheart, that reporter Baker? He did a story about the hearing yesterday. You don't need to read it."

She felt a stirring of irritation. Setting her black mug down on the table she said, "Edward Austin Stanton, what is going on?"

"Megan," there was a note of pleading in his voice. "The article will only upset you. I'm just trying to protect you."

"I don't need to be protected," Megan snapped. She went to the small kitchen trash can under the sink and checked it. No newspaper. "Where did you pitch it?"

Ed got to his feet. "Honey, you don't want to read it."

"Yes I do!" she replied. "What are you hiding?"

He closed his eyes and sighed. "Sweetheart, we haven't talked about what you said in your statement yesterday...I didn't have the energy to talk about it, or the heart..."

"What are you trying to say?" Megan asked. She realized that they hadn't spoken very much to each other after the hearing – she'd been too wrapped up in her grief to speak much about it and assumed Ed was the same.

Ed rubbed his eyes. "Megan, you said you wanted that boy to go to Hell."

"Well, shouldn't he?" she demanded. "Isn't that what he deserves, after what he did?"

"Which of us doesn't deserve it?" Ed countered, getting to his feet. "All of us need God's grace."

Megan felt her jaw drop. "You and I – we're nothing like that creature!"

"We're all sinners," Ed replied. "I've been talking to Jack about this...I've been so angry, Megan, and I didn't want to be. I see it in you as well."

"We have every right to be angry!" Megan said. "He murdered our child!"

"He didn't mean to," Ed said. "It was an accident."

"No!" she shook her head. Tears sprang to her eyes. "It doesn't matter – he still killed her. I can't forgive that. Can you?"

Ed dropped his gaze to the faded green linoleum. In a voice almost too soft for her to hear, he said, "I want to."

For a moment she felt as if Ed had reached over and slapped her. She stumbled back a couple of steps, then leaned against the kitchen sink. "You can't mean that."

"I do," Ed said. His Adam's apple bobbed as he swallowed. "I – I've been praying for Morrison. Jack said it would help. I'm not there yet – but I'm starting to feel that I can let go of the hate –"

"What about Anna?" Megan said, her voice breaking. "What about our baby?"

Ed raised his head to look at her. "Hating that boy won't bring Anna back."

Megan tore her gaze from her husband and looked out the window over the sink. The day was overcast, a light breeze rippling through the sturdy oak tree in the backyard. A treehouse nestled in its branches. Anna had loved spending time there, reading, giggling with girlfriends, playing...

"How can you even think about forgiving that monster?" she hissed. "It's like you don't care about what he did to our daughter."

She heard him gasp and wished at once she could call back her hasty words. She looked over at him and saw the hurt and anger etched on his face. There were lines that hadn't been there two months ago.

Anna's death had taken its toll on him too. How could she have forgotten that?

"I'm sorry," she stammered. "I shouldn't have –"

He held up a hand to stop her. "Don't. Not now. I – I can't talk to you right now."

"Ed, please, I'm sorry!" She reached out for him but he took a step back, glancing at his watch.

"I told Sam I'd come into work today – I need to get going," he said, avoiding her gaze. "I'll see you later."

She felt panic tightening her chest. "Ed, please, we shouldn't leave it like this. Don't leave me like this."

He took a deep breath. "Megan, I love you – but you're letting your hatred of this boy consume you. If you don't stop it, there'll be nothing left of you."

She opened her mouth to protest but he raised a hand, silencing her. "I'm going to go to work. Think about it. Pray about it. I promise we'll talk more later, but right now – you hurt me, Megan, and I'm afraid I'll say something I shouldn't if I don't leave."

She huffed, hurt and confused by her husband's words. "Well, fine then. Go."

The sadness in his eyes brought tears to her own. He came to her and kissed her cheek. "I love you," he murmured. Then he left her in the kitchen, alone with her roiling emotions.

She stood by the sink until she heard the door leading to the garage shut. Then she buried her face in her hands and wept.

After she straightened up the kitchen, Megan found herself standing outside of Anna's room. She hesitated, a hand on the doorknob, the other holding her now cold cup of coffee.

She hadn't been in the room since the day she'd had to select a dress to send to the funeral home for her dead daughter. Megan closed her eyes against the memory. She'd barely been able to see through her tears. Jack's wife Sharon had been there and together they'd picked out a forest green dress with a full skirt that Anna had loved.

After that Megan had simply shut the door and refused to enter the room again. She wondered if Ed had gone in since that day – it wasn't something they discussed. Megan had the uncomfortable feeling that there were a number of things they hadn't discussed since the night they'd gotten the phone call from the hospital.

But now...Megan felt an overwhelming need to connect

with her daughter. Things seemed so wrong at the moment, maybe this would help her make sense of what was going on.

With that thought, she turned the knob and pushed the door open. Bracing herself, she took a couple of steps into the room, scanning it with her eyes.

The first thing that struck her was how normal the room looked. The four-poster bed was made, covered with a blue and white quilt that Megan's mother had sewn. Fuzzy pale blue slippers by the side of the bed, on top of a small red Oriental rug.

Megan swallowed. She could almost see Anna sprawled out on the bed, feet waving in the air as she texted one of her many friends. Or maybe sitting at the cherry wood desk that sat across from the bed, working on some homework assignment on her laptop computer.

The laptop wasn't there now – Anna had it with her when she died.

Megan noticed that Anna's Bible was sitting on a corner of the desk. The dark red cover had her name in gold on the bottom right-hand corner. A thin layer of dust covered the book and the desk, reminding Megan that no one had been in this room for a while.

Blinking back tears, she picked up the Bible, placing her coffee cup on the desk. The one faint comfort she had in this nightmare was the confidence that her daughter was safe in Heaven. She began to leaf through the book, noting passages here and there that her daughter had marked with a yellow highlighter.

When she got to the book of Matthew, her gaze was drawn to a passage that was not only highlighted, but had the word "wow" scrawled in the margin beside it. Curious, she read the verses: *For if ye forgive men their trespasses, your heavenly Father will also forgive you: But if ye forgive not men their trespasses, neither will your Father forgive your trespasses.*

With a gasp, Megan slapped the Bible closed. She flung it back onto the desk and took a step back, her heart pounding hard against her chest. She stared at the leather-bound book as if it might suddenly start speaking to her, condemning her.

"No," she whispered. Didn't God understand? Did He know what He was asking of her? What about her pain? Her suffering? Her overwhelming loss?

When the doorbell rang, she jumped. Settle down, she told herself angrily. It was probably someone wanting to offer support and make sure she was okay. Or maybe it was Jack Peters, wanting to have that talk he mentioned yesterday.

The bell rang a second time. Megan grabbed her coffee cup off the desk and left the room with rapid steps, shutting the door firmly behind her. On the way to answer the front door she stopped in the guest bathroom to check her appearance. Her eyes were red-rimmed and shadowed, but there were no traces of tears. Deciding she looked as good as she was going to, she went to the front door.

The woman standing on Megan's doorstep had graying curly brown hair and a nervous expression. She wore a wrinkled floral print shirt and cranberry color pants. "Mrs. Stanton?"

The woman looked familiar, but Megan couldn't immediately place her. But something about her made Megan uncomfortable. "Yes? Can I help you?"

The woman gripped the strap of her black shoulder bag. "I – I'm Rebecca Morrison. I saw you in court yesterday."

Megan caught her breath. This woman had sat behind

the killer's table, had embraced him afterwards. She was the one who'd looked at Megan with compassion...

Megan's first impulse was to slam the door in this woman's face. Her hand tightened on the edge of the door as her thoughts raced. "You – you're his mother?" she ground out.

"Yes," the woman nodded. "Please, can I talk to you? I know I have no right, but – please?"

Megan shook her head before the woman finished speaking. "I don't have anything to say to you. I'm sorry."

"But I need to speak with you. Please," the woman begged, her pale blue eyes swimming with tears. "Please, I won't be long..."

"Did *he* send you?" Megan demanded.

"Not exactly," the curly haired woman said. "I'm trying to – to help him do the right thing. Please Mrs. Stanton, I know you must hate me, but all I want is a few minutes of your time."

Megan froze. Did she hate Rebecca Morrison? She considered that for a moment. What, really, had this sad woman done to her? She had nothing to do with her son's actions. Was Megan really so consumed with hatred for her daughter's killer that she would extend it to innocent members of his family?

Rebecca Morrison said nothing more, just stood there gazing at Megan with a pleading expression. Her hands twisted the strap of her shoulder bag and Megan noticed the other woman's knuckles were white.

Swallowing, Megan took a step back and said, "Come in, please."

She watched the killer's mother take a deep breath and then step inside. Megan shut the door behind her. Uncertain of what she should do, she gestured to her coffee cup.

"Would you like some coffee? I think there's some left over from breakfast."

Clearing her throat, her guest said, "That would be nice, thank you."

Megan led the way into the kitchen. She waved towards the breakfast nook. "Have a seat. How do you take your coffee?"

Mrs. Morrison hung her purse over the back of a chair and sat. "Black is fine."

"All right." Megan dumped her cold coffee and got a clean white mug from a nearby cupboard for her guest. It didn't take long before the two women were sitting across from each other, mugs of coffee in front of them.

The silence between them stretched like a taut rubber band. Megan felt herself growing more tense with each passing moment. She gripped her mug so hard she was surprised it didn't shatter in her hands.

Mrs. Morrison gazed into her own drink, not looking up. Megan wondered if she'd taken the other woman by surprise by letting her in and now she didn't know what to do.

Finally she decided enough was enough. "You said you wanted to speak with me, Mrs. Morrison?"

The other woman jerked, nearly spilling her coffee. "Please, call me Rebecca."

"Fine," Megan said. "What did you want to talk about, Rebecca?"

Rebecca sighed. "About Patrick, if you'll allow it."

Megan felt her defenses going up. "I don't care about him."

"Yes, you've made that quite clear," Rebecca replied. "Mrs. Stanton, I won't sit here and say I know what you're going through...if one of my children died I don't know what I'd do..."

She stopped and took a sip of coffee. "It's just that... Patrick is in agony. He is such a gentle person, he wouldn't deliberately hurt anyone –"

"But he did," Megan interrupted. "And he should be suffering for it. Don't try to excuse what he did."

"I'm not," Rebecca answered. "It was stupid and careless and he is going to have to live with it the rest of his life. He's going to jail. But isn't that punishment enough?"

"Enough?" Megan pushed away from the table and began to pace. "Ten years. He gets his life back in ten years! How is that enough?"

"No," Rebecca argued. "He will never get his life back to what it was. He can't undo what happened, and it's killed a part of him that he can't. He has nightmares about the accident, did you know that?"

"I don't care," Megan said, stopping to glare at Rebecca. "Do you want to talk about nightmares? My *life* is a nightmare, thanks to him! I've lost my only child. Don't you understand that?"

"But it was an accident," Rebecca said, her tears overflowing. "If you'd just talk to him, you'd see how heartbroken he is. He didn't mean for it to happen!"

"And that makes it all right?" Megan demanded. "My daughter is still dead."

Rebecca closed her eyes. "This was a mistake," she murmured. "I hoped you would understand...that you were a compassionate woman who could see past your grief."

"What do you want from me?" Megan cried. "He's the one who's guilty here, why should I give him anything?"

Rebecca stood and picked up her purse. "I want...never

mind. You clearly meant what you said yesterday." She wiped her eyes. "Thank you for the coffee. I'll leave."

Megan found herself in a strange conflict. She felt as if Rebecca Morrison had judged her and found her wanting somehow. It shouldn't have hurt, but it did.

Rebecca was at the doorway to the kitchen when she stopped. She kept her back to Megan. "You mentioned God yesterday, Mrs. Stanton. I hope He shows you more mercy than you're willing to show others."

... if ye forgive not men their trespasses, neither will your Father forgive your trespasses.

Megan froze, the words of the Bible verse echoing in her head. By the time she found her voice, the front door was closing. She hurried over to it and yanked it open in time to see Rebecca unlocking a green Honda Accord.

Part of her wanted to let the woman get out of her life. But her parting words troubled Megan. "Rebecca," she called out.

The curly-haired woman paused, her hand on the car door. She gazed at Megan, saying nothing.

Megan struggled to come up with words to explain the storm of emotions that roiled inside of her. Anger was certainly there, and grief never fully went away. But now guilt had shown up for the party – fueled by the feeling that in spite of everything, she might be wrong.

She saw Rebecca sigh and start to slide into the car. Realizing she'd just been standing there saying nothing she hurried over to the Honda. "Wait, please."

Rebecca started the engine, then turned to face Megan. "Yes?"

Megan clasped her shaking hands together. "I'm – I'm sorry that you seem to think I'm heartless. What you're asking me to do – what everyone seems to want me to do – I don't know if I'm strong enough to."

"Just talk to him," Rebecca said. "Before you condemn him – please, go and talk to him."

Megan swallowed. Go to her daughter's killer? Visit him in prison, a place she'd never gone? And...then what?

As if reading her mind, Rebecca spoke in a soft voice. "I realize you might still hate Patrick after you see him. But at least he'll be a person to you then – not just a murderer."

Megan studied her clasped hands. "I...I don't know."

"You are on the list of approved visitors," Rebecca told her. "Both you and your husband. Patrick requested it. If you want to see him, you can."

"I have to think about it," Megan said. The sunlight faded and she glanced up. The clouds were scurrying across the sky, their gray color warning her of coming rain. A light breeze kicked up and Megan smelled the sharp odor that sometimes preceded a storm.

Rebecca noticed the change in the weather as well. "Whatever you decide, Mrs. Stanton, know my family is sorry for your loss and we hope you find peace."

Megan glanced down at Rebecca. "Thank you," she said, because the situation seemed to demand the words.

"You're welcome." Rebecca reached over for the car door as Megan stepped back, allowing the curly-haired woman to shut it. Megan watched the car back out of her driveway and set off down the street.

She was still looking that way, lost in thought, when the first fat raindrops started falling.

A week went by before Megan worked up the nerve to drive to the prison. During that time, she'd argued with herself and with God, going back and forth on the issue. One minute she'd decide that Rebecca Morrison was manipulative and didn't deserve the time of day, much less Megan visiting her son. The next she'd ask herself something like what would Jesus do, and the answer always seemed to point to a visit to the prison.

She hadn't told Ed about Rebecca's visit. When he arrived home from work that day she'd apologized again, and he seemed to accept that. But neither of them brought up the hearing or the killer. Megan sensed that Ed was giving her space to sort out her thoughts and feelings, and she appreciated that, especially given what she was contemplating.

The morning of the visit was bright and humid. Megan used her phone's GPS to get directions to the prison, located in an adjoining county. She treated herself to a fast food breakfast on the way, nibbling the ham, egg, and cheese biscuit as she drove.

Several times she almost turned back. But then she'd glance at the seat beside her, where Anna's Bible rested. Somehow, she thought that her daughter would want her to do this, and the leather-covered book reminded Megan of the faith she shared with her child. She prayed that faith would see her through this visit.

The state prison was depressing. The fences, the concrete block buildings, the guards – it all seemed designed to suck the confidence and optimism out of a person. As she pulled into the parking lot set aside for visitors Megan tried to imagine having to stay in this place.

Remembering what she'd read on the prison's webpage, she locked her purse in the trunk of her car. She wished she could carry in Anna's Bible with her, but the instructions she'd read had been clear – no books.

"The Lord is my shepherd," she murmured to herself as she walked towards the visitor's entrance. "I shall not want…"

As Megan went through the process of putting her phone on a conveyor belt to be scanned and walking through a metal detector, she recited the rest of the psalm to herself. It helped remind her that God was still with her, even in this awful place.

Before too long she was seated in a cubicle in front of a scratched glass window. A telephone receiver was to her right and she saw another one on the other side. She shifted in the uncomfortable folding chair and waited.

When Anna's killer walked into the room on the other side of the glass, Megan felt a sense of shock go through her. He was pale, and his brown hair was disheveled. A shiner decorated his left eye, and the orange jumpsuit he wore looked too big on his frame.

He didn't look like a monster at all.

His good eye widened when he saw Megan. He slid into the chair opposite her and lifted the black receiver on his side of the window. Swallowing, Megan picked up her own receiver and held it to her ear.

"Mrs. Stanton?" His voice shook a little. "Thanks for coming."

Megan stared at him. She tried to think of when she'd seen someone look so defeated before. His shoulders slumped as he sat in front of her, waiting for her to say something.

When she found her voice, she asked, "What happened to your eye?"

"Oh," he said, raising a hand to the swollen part of his face. "It's nothing. I just got someone mad at me."

Megan gripped the receiver tightly, her other hand balled into a fist under the scarred beige counter in front of her. She prayed silently, *Lord, give me the words.* Her mind was blank. The awful things she'd considered hurling at this young man...they seemed so pointless.

They sat in silence for a long moment. Megan caught snatches of conversations on either side of her as she fought conflicting emotions.

He broke the silence first. "I know this must be hard for you."

"It is," she agreed. "But I feel I needed to come."

She heard his chair creak faintly as he shifted in it. "I...I know you hate me. And I deserve it. I just...I just wanted you to know that I didn't mean for it to happen. I wish I could take it back. I'm so sorry...but I guess that's not enough, is it?"

Megan closed her eyes. Her grief rose up like a wave and crashed over her, filling her with sorrow. But the anger she'd come to expect and almost welcome was absent.

She opened her eyes and looked at him. It was almost as if she were seeing him for the first time. This wasn't some heartless, faceless killer. This was a boy. A boy who was in pain.

Megan realized he was waiting for her to respond to his question. "I...I don't know what you want me to say."

His eyes welled up. "I just hope...is there a chance you'll ever forgive me? Maybe someday?"

Biting her lip, she faced the question. That's what this all came down to, wasn't it? Could she forgive Morrison for what he'd done? For what he'd taken from her?

Love your enemies.

She sighed. There was only one answer she could honestly give. "I don't know."

His face fell and he dropped his gaze to the counter in front of him, where a tear splashed. Megan felt she needed to explain. "Please understand – I *want* to forgive you. I know that I need to as a Christian. But...right now it's very hard."

He nodded, not raising up his eyes to her. More tears joined the first on the counter.

To Megan's surprise, she felt a stab of pity for Morrison. She scoured her mind for something she could say or do, some simple step she could take...

The idea came to her, and she hesitated. But it wouldn't leave her mind. "Mr. Morrison..." No. That sounded too formal, too distant. "Patrick?"

He glanced up, wiping his eyes with the back of his hand. "Yes ma'am?"

Megan tried to relax her tense shoulders. "Do you have a Bible?"

The question seemed to surprise him. He shrugged. "I have one at home. There's Bibles in the library here. I...I have to admit I don't go to church. My parents, they go, but I haven't been in a while."

Megan nodded. "If I gave you Anna's Bible, would you promise to read it every day?"

His eyes widened. "I don't want to take your daughter's Bible, Mrs. Stanton."

"That's not what I asked," Megan pressed. "If you had it, would you read it?"

He stared at her for a long moment. Megan snuck a glance at her watch – their time was almost up. What if he turned her down? What if he mocked her for her gesture?

In a low voice, Morrison said, "I will read it. Every day like you said. Only...I don't know where to start."

Megan's shoulders sagged in relief and a little sorrow. "All right. I'll send it to you. You can start with the Gospels – they tell the story of Jesus. And if you have any questions, you can write me and I'll try to answer them."

"You'll do that?" Morrison asked. "I can write you?"

"Yes," Megan said. A harsh buzzer sounded and she knew their time was up. "Remember, you said you'd read it every day."

Morrison nodded. "I will. I promise." He noticed a guard approaching and quickly added, "Thank you." He then hung up the receiver and rose from his chair, following the guard out. Megan couldn't help but notice that he seemed a little more confident as he left, as if a weight had been removed from him.

She made her way back to the parking lot, the heat and humidity striking her like a blow after being in the rather chilly prison. Megan hurried to her car and got in, welcoming the air conditioning that poured out of the vents.

Anna's Bible still sat in the passenger seat. Megan regarded it with a pang. It cost her to give it up. But something told her that Patrick Morrison needed this particular Bible far more than she did.

Remembering something Ed had said a week ago, Megan realized there was something else she could do. Forgiveness would take time. But perhaps, along with opening the door to sharing God's word with the boy, there was something else she could do to help set her on the right path.

Resting her hands on the steering wheel, Megan bowed her head and for the first time prayed for Patrick Morrison.

ALSO BY LAURA WARE

www.ingramcontent.com/pod-product-compliance
Lightning Source LLC
Chambersburg PA
CBHW022039170626
46808CB00003B/1282